ALEX GARLAND

The Tesseract

VIKING

VIKING

Published by the Penguin Group
Penguin Books Ltd, 27 Wrights Lane, London w8 5tz, England
Penguin Putnam Inc., 375 Hudson Street, New York, New York 10014, USA
Penguin Books Australia Ltd, Ringwood, Victoria, Australia
Penguin Books Canada Ltd, 10 Alcorn Avenue, Toronto, Ontario, Canada m4v 3b2
Penguin Books (NZ) Ltd, Private Bag 102902, NSMC, Auckland, New Zealand

Penguin Books Ltd, Registered Offices: Harmondsworth, Middlesex, England

First published in Great Britain by Viking 1998
1 3 5 7 9 10 8 6 4 2
First edition

Filmset in 12/14pt Monotype Fournier by Intype London Ltd
Printed in Great Britain by Clays Ltd, St Ives plc

A CIP catalogue record for this book is available from the British Library

ISBN 0–670–870153
ISBN 0–670–870161

For Paloma, Richard and Dimitri, Rey, Garcie, James, and the same people as the first book.

'The larger the searchlight, the larger the circumference of the unknown'

DICK TAYLOR

I—I

Black Dog

I

There was no bright colour in the room.

Outside there was plenty. Through the bars of his window, Sean could see sunlight on drifting litter and flashes of foliage in the narrow gaps between squatter shacks. But inside, nothing. Beige and khaki, faded by age, muted by the hopelessly dim bulbs that sat on each side of his bed.

'Stains,' said Sean under his breath. It was something that the hotel room had in common with the street two storeys below. In both places, there wasn't a single surface without some kind of grubby scar, everything marked by rain or dust, smoke, the overspill from the open sewers, the open fires that burned on the pavement. And blood. There was blood on the bedsheets. The spatter had paled from a few hard scrubs, but it was still rustily recognizable for what it was.

'Heat.'

The other thing that his room shared with the city. Oozing out from the sun, heat like molasses. Once it had touched you, you were stuck with it.

It had touched Sean that afternoon as he sat on Manila Bay's low harbour wall, looking out at the cargo ships and their fat anchor chains. Up to then he'd been protected by the reassuring air-con of an Ermita McDonald's. He'd gone there for breakfast, around ten a.m., with a copy of *Asia Week* rolled in his fist. At eleven fifteen he'd stood up to leave and walked towards the

3

exit, where the blue-uniformed McDonald's security guard had obligingly lowered his stockless shot-gun and held the door open. Or obligingly held the door open and lowered his stockless shot-gun. Either way, one blast from the scorched air and Sean had spun on his heels and marched back inside.

But cool as it was in McDonald's, after a couple of hours Sean could feel the edges of his mind starting to fray. It wasn't the obsessive wiping and washing and ashtray-removing so much as the sprawling children's party that had commandeered half the seating area. Overweight rich kids with sulky faces and stripy sailors' shirts, shouting at their nannies. No more than eight or nine, most of them, and already groomed for a life in politics. Why did this tubby élite choose to celebrate in a hamburger joint, Sean had wondered as he burst a balloon that had been bounced into his face. The sound made a dozen adult heads turn and had one of the minders reaching under his *barong tagalog* to the bulge in his waistband. So, time to go.

Armed with a milkshake, Sean had left the McDonald's and walked to the waterfront, where he'd hoped he might kill time in the company of a cool sea breeze. But there was no cool sea breeze. There was an executive-bathroom hand-drier blowing down his neck. The milkshake had turned to chocolate soup before it was even a quarter finished, the bench he'd chosen was like leaning against an oven door, and the sparse canopies of the palm trees offered nothing more than a rumour of shade.

Yet somehow, Sean had managed to stick it out until four. He couldn't remember much about how the time had passed, he was simply glad that it had. Ships and water were good for distracting a head that needed to be distracted. Good for a blink and a mild frown, and a glance at a watch that said half an hour had swept by. Sean's only clear memory of the afternoon was standing on the harbour wall and looking down at the beached jellyfish and acres of floating refuse. Like little islands, he'd thought, watching the polystyrene chips and plastic bags that bobbed in the swell. There are two archipelagos beneath me. One too big to think about, and the other too big to see.

Back in his room, some of the wetter stains on the street had begun to glow red as the sun dropped from the sky. Dropped, because the sun didn't sink in these parts. At six fifteen, the elastic that kept it suspended started to stretch, and at six thirty, the elastic snapped. Then you had just ten minutes as the orange ellipse plummeted out of view, and the next thing you knew it was night. You had to watch out for that in Manila. Ten minutes to catch a cab to the right side of town if you were on the wrong side.

'Like now, for example,' Sean murmured, as the red puddles blackened and disappeared. Miles from Ermita or any place he knew, holed up in a hotel that didn't know it was a hotel, or had forgotten.

No other guests. No air-con or even a fan. No lobby. Just a chair and a desk and a man downstairs, his T-shirt always rolled up to his chest and a belly like a brown boulder. A man who usually had a sweat-soaked cigarette tucked between his right ear and the stubble of his shaved head. A man who kept one hand permanently out of view and never returned Sean's smile, simply slid his key towards him with a flick of the fingers.

What sort of hotel had no other guests? Walking down the corridor, through flickering pools of light where there were bulbs instead of hanging wires, Sean had noticed the quiet with growing confusion. He'd also seen open doors, and through them rooms without beds. Sometimes rooms without walls. Only a few wooden slats, the guts of the walls, or the bones. And past the bones, the neighbouring room, equally bare and broken.

Everything weird was the bottom line, and Sean had reached

it quickly. Within an hour of his arrival, everything weird — every corner, every noise, every object.

The telephone, sitting on his arthritic bedside table. It didn't work. Of course it didn't work. If the hotel management weren't bothered about missing walls, they were unlikely to care about telephones. But whether it worked or not, did it have to be so mysteriously burned? Cigarette burns, and not from carelessly held butts. These were in patterns, lines and curls. These were the results of someone practising their torturing skills. Sean had known it as surely as he'd known that the line would be dead. Known it, but refused to accept it until he'd spent five minutes listening to the utter lack of dial tone, pushing the receiver button and jiggling the base in the hope of provoking a little static.

Sean had needed three Temazepam to get to sleep that first night. And he'd read over the address he'd been given as compulsively as he'd smoked, examining the bit of paper for anything that resembled an ambiguity. Screwing up his eyes, Sean had tried to read 'Alejandro Street' as 'Alejandra Street', or 'Hotel Patay' as 'Hotel Ratay'. He'd tried even after the sleeping pills had dissolved his focus and his lips were too numb to pull on a cigarette. He'd tried in his sleep, his dream a liquid continuation of the preceding hours.

So difficult to believe he was in the right place. 'Patay' being 'patay', difficult to believe. But he was in the right place. The next morning, Sean discovered that a note had been left at reception. Don Pepe's elaborate handwriting, confirming their meeting at eight o'clock the coming night. A meeting that was now exactly sixty-eight minutes away, assuming the *mestizo* arrived on time.

2

At seven o'clock, Sean moved away from the window. Dark room to a light street, you see everything, but dark street to a light room, you see nothing and everything sees you. So Sean moved away from the window and sat on his bed.

He wasn't feeling good. The sun, the long afternoon on the low harbour wall, had left him drained and dehydrated. Irritable, if there'd been anyone to be irritable with; jumpy, seeing as he was alone. And the waiting didn't help. It made Sean tense at the best of times, hanging on someone else's arrival. In general he organized meetings so that he was the one arriving, particularly in places where lack of punctuality was a source of national pride. But in this case, Sean had acquiesced to the arrangement Don Pepe requested. Acquiesced in the way you acquiesce to a tank, requested in the way a tank requests you move out of its path.

No, that wasn't quite right. Don Pepe was tank-like only to the degree that he made Sean feel powerless. Past that the similarity ended. He wasn't a large man, slighter than the average Filipino, and he didn't blunder or shout or even raise his voice. He just nodded and smiled, and sapped will like a hot bath.

Sean sighed and lit a cigarette.

Odd, nicotine. At the moment Sean lit up, he'd been gazing vacantly into space. One drag on the cigarette and his gaze zoned straight to the spyhole – straight like a zoom lens, nicotine clarity. The spyhole was blocked.

For some reason, there was a small steel plate screwed over it on the corridor side, and judging by the silver scratch-marks on the metal, the plate had been placed there recently. Fairly recently. More than forty-eight hours, because he'd noticed it when he first saw his room.

He hadn't been worried about it back then. Relative to everything else in the hotel, the blocked spyhole had seemed pretty inconsequential. Now it seemed different. It seemed strange. Three or four drags into his cigarette, it occurred to Sean that blocking the spyhole couldn't be of any benefit to guests. Couldn't ever be good, not knowing who was knocking at the door. In fact, the only person who could benefit would be someone outside the room.

At the expense of the person inside. That was what was strange.

Sean frowned. Removing it would be two minutes' work. He could get out his Swiss Army knife, fiddle around a bit, and the strange thing would be history. The hotel would be marginally less strange.

He stared at the tiny useless circle, but stayed on the bed. Not about to get paranoid, beaten by sun on a harbour wall and a few hours waiting in a weird hotel. If it hadn't bothered him last night, it wasn't going to bother him now. And anyway, it wasn't like spyholes were such a lot of use. You hear someone at the door, you go to check who it is, you don't want to see them, what do you do? Not answer? Chances are they've heard you as you walk across the room, so you can't pretend you're out. And if it's trouble, the best you can do is slip the chain on the lock. Which buys as much time as one hard kick.

The cigarette was down to the filter. Sean watched the red glow eat into the butt for a couple of seconds, then he stubbed it out.

Nine past seven, nine minutes since he last looked at his watch. Nine times sixty seconds. Easy. Ten times sixty minus sixty equals five hundred and forty seconds, just under one-sixth of the time before the *mestizo* turned up, assuming he was on time, which meant there were fifty-one times sixty seconds to go, which was . . .

A cockroach zipped across the carpet like a miniature skateboard.

The rats and mosquitoes had packed their bags and checked out. With a city-wide network of slums on the doorstep, there was no sense in hunting for food scraps or skin. A parasite could afford to be choosy. But the cockroaches had decided that the hotel still had something to offer. They'd stuck around, multiplied like crazy, seething in the gap between the mattress base and the floor, slipping through the vent of the long-dead air-con unit. Completely indifferent to everything, happy in a pile of shit. Hard to find a creature that cared for the company of cockroaches, hard to find a cockroach that cared.

Hard to kill, too. Corner them with a lighter flame and they strolled through the flame, whack them with a newspaper and they laughed in your face. The creature best suited to life after the bomb. Amazing, to be able to cope with atomic fall-out so well, and a shoe heel so badly.

Sean slid off the bed.

Seven seventeen, four dead roaches, flattened, burst, floating in the toilet bowl; the world a better place.

The flush made Sean wince and tap his foot impatiently while the cistern refilled. The noise was as loud and awkward as a cough at a funeral. Noise didn't belong in Patay. The quiet inside the hotel was so absolute that it appeared to have infected the street outside. Unprecedented in the city, cars and jeepneys laid off the horns when passing, motorbikes eased off the throttle, *balut* vendors didn't bother calling out. The rest of Manila rippled with these sounds twenty-four hours a day, but not Alejandro Street. Patay existed in a cocoon of silence.

Virtual silence. Sometimes it was broken. Curious sounds,

difficult to place, unnaturally amplified and confused by the vacuum around them. Trapped air in the water pipes that sounded like footsteps, barking dogs that sounded like crashing cars.

Two of the roaches didn't make it down the U-bend. One turned out to be still alive, struggling with the surface tension and its leaking innards. Brown innards, Sean noticed, thoughtfully thumbing the sweat out of his eyebrows. So sure enough, you are what you eat.

Clarity – maybe.

Back on the bed, Sean lay with his head propped up on his elbow, looking at the blood on the sheets. He thought to himself: connections. The telephone, the blood-stained sheets and the spyhole. The three things came out of nowhere, they were *non sequiturs*. But nothing comes out of nowhere and *non sequiturs* don't exist. There had to be a connection.

Sean traced around the rusty spatter with his finger.

Start at the beginning. There had been someone staying in the room, obviously. And judging by the phone, the someone was a torturer, possibly by trade. Which, more than likely, made the person a man. So, a man in a room, and a room that smelled of melted plastic. A blue haze clinging to the ceiling. A full pack of cigarettes in the ashtray, burned down to the butts.

The man was breathing that smoke, smelling that smell, when he heard the sound of screws turning, splintering the dry wood as they pushed into the door.

He sat up abruptly, cocked his head to hear better. He looked around the room with widening eyes until he pinpointed the source. Then he stood, taking care to move quietly, and padded over to the spyhole. He peered through. He saw only blackness.

He'd have asked himself, what was out there that he shouldn't see? What was passing or arriving?

Probably he'd have slipped the chain on the door to buy the

hard-kick time. Carefully, because, in Patay or anywhere else, no noise carries like scraping metal. Then over to the bars on the window to give them a tug. No joy there, sunk deep into the concrete, about the only things in the hotel that did the job they were meant for. Then into the bathroom to see the width of the air vent. Way too narrow. A macaque monkey could barely have squeezed in.

He abandoned stealth. He probably had a gun. He went to get it, put it in his hand if it wasn't there already.

With the spyhole blocked, he didn't know how many were on the other side of his door. But he knew he was stuck in the room and there were going to be enough outside to get him, gun or no gun. As a torturer, he knew exactly what that meant. He was familiar with that scene.

So that was the thing – he was familiar. He went back across to the bed, sat down, and blew his brains all over the sheets.

'A shaving accident,' said Sean. 'An unexpected menstruation. A nosebleed. A miscarriage.' His throat hurt from too much tobacco. He lit another cigarette off the stub of the last one.

Seven twenty-four. Sean had often heard people joke about the number of blades on Swiss Army knives, how no one could ever find a use for all of them. But Sean had found a use for all his blades within the first two months of purchase, and sometimes wished the knife had a few more.

He worked as quickly as he could. He'd had to close the door in order to have something to push against while he unscrewed the plate, and he felt exposed in the corridor. It gave him the creeps.

3

The steel plate was purpose-made. About the size of a playing card, around the thickness of a door key, with edges still rough from the hacksaw. Unfiled and sharp enough to cut a finger.

Its purpose had ended. Sean closed his door behind him and made as if he were about to chuck it on to the bed, but instead he threw it at the wall. A flash of anger had hit him as he'd pulled back his hand, irritation at having been beaten by the sun after all. The steel plate spun towards the rotten plasterboard and sank in like a throwing knife.

Immediately an alarm sounded, an urgent buzzing that filled the room, breaking on and off without rhythm.

At first Sean was too surprised to react. Then he lunged forwards and pulled the plate out. He thought he must have severed a wire, triggering an arcane fire-warning system.

The alarm continued to sound. The wires had to be rejoined, quickly, before the shaven-headed receptionist came to investigate. But seconds later, clawing rubble from the hole he'd just punched, Sean saw that there were no wires. The walls were hollow. No brickwork, just wooden slats and the smell of trapped air. And bizarrely, the buzzing seemed to have become even more urgent. The rhythm was less regular and the gaps between the buzzes were shorter.

He dithered, stupidly tugging at the torn wallpaper, then realized that if there were no wires, the steel plate was irrelevant. In which case, there actually *was* a fire. Sean swore and darted back across his room to his bag, imagining the speed at which flames would rip through the old hotel.

He stopped as he passed his bedside table.

It was the phone. The *phone* was ringing.

*

'Aaaaah . . . Hello, Sean.'

Sean gripped the receiver hard. He told himself: no time for shock.

Keeping his voice steady, catching his breath between words, he said, 'Don Pepe! Hi! *Kumusta po kayon?*'

Don Pepe made a sucking sound. He was chewing a matchstick, as he always did. His matchstick was one of his weapons. Ask him a question and he'd suck his fucking matchstick, always making you wait for the answer.

'*Kumusta ka*, Don Pepe,' Sean repeated, in an attempt to cut the mind-game out before it started, but the sucking continued. Don Pepe wouldn't speak until he was ready.

'Well, Sean,' he eventually said. 'Eeeeh, I'm okay *lang*. How about you?'

'I'm fine. Okay, *din po*.'

'Okay, *din* . . .' Suck. 'You like the hotel?'

Sean smoothed down the damp cotton of his shirt. 'It's quiet.'

'Yes, quiet. But, you know, Sean, I made a mistake. Last year the hotel was, *ano*, a bery good hotel. But now my associate tells me it is palling down already. This was my mistake. I thought it was still a good hotel.'

'Oh, you didn't know,' said Sean, hardly able to keep the disbelief out of his voice. 'Really.'

'*Talaga. Pero*, if we are meeting in only tirty minutes, eeeh, it's already too late to change, *di ba?*'

'Well . . . Maybe it's not too late. We could meet in a bar. We could meet in . . .' Sean paused to think of somewhere public and open. 'We could meet in the Penguin bar. I could get to Ermita in half an hour. It would be easy. *Madeli po.*'

This time the sucking lasted for at least twenty seconds. Sean gripped the receiver a little more tightly each time a smacked lip crackled down the phone line. He was determined not be the one to break the silence. But when his knuckles were the colour of his teeth, he heard himself saying, 'Maybe we should just meet in the hotel, Don Pepe.'

'Yes,' said Don Pepe. 'Let's just meet in the hotel. I think it will be easier, and we will have the pribacy to talk.'

'Yes.'

'So anyway, aaaah, I was really teleponing to let you know, I will be, *ano*, a little bit late por our meeting.'

' . . . Late?'

'Yes.'

'Uh, okay . . . How late?'

'Maybe pipteen minutes. One quarter ob an hour. That's *ayos*?'

'*Ayos na*. No problem, *po*.'

'Okay, so, aaaah, eeeeh, good. See you then.'

'*Sige po.*'

'*Sige.*'

Don Pepe put the phone down.

The dial tone stayed for six or seven seconds, then the line went dead.

Sean struggled with himself. He was trying to neaten the hole he'd made, trying to pat the wallpaper back over the gap. It wasn't possible. His hands were shaking too much. They contradicted themselves, the fingers feeling fat and clumsy, the steady tremble feeling tentative and delicate. Helpless, he found he was only adding to the rips. In a burst of frustration he tore off a strip clean down to the skirting board.

'I'm losing,' Sean said, stepping away from the spreading disaster area.

No question, but spoken out loud it sounded like a revelation.

For a few moments, Patay was in perspective. He had arranged to meet a man in a hotel, and the man was coming. Past that nothing had happened, nothing had gone wrong. During those moments, the furniture was teak. Beneath the grime, the lamp fittings and curtain rings were brass. The headboard on the bed was hand carved, a relief of coconut trees and fishermen and nipa huts. He was standing in faded splendour.

Then his vision clouded. Teak was a crime and fishermen were poor. Arranged to meet a man whose name was a black joke, told quietly in bars around Manila. *Don Pepe's prayer before he sleeps? Forgive me, Father, for I am sin.* If Don Pepe slept at all.

Dropping to his knees, Sean grabbed his overnight bag and jerked open the zip. A change of clothes spilled on to the carpet, followed by a pair of sunglasses he never wore and a fresh pack of cigarettes.

'Come on,' Sean hissed. He gave the bag a shake. A toothbrush joined the pile, then a single AA battery, then a spare magazine. He paused to put the magazine to the side before shaking the bag again. A ballpoint pen, some loose coins, some loose shells, a flashlight, another AA battery and a charm.

4

Only a charm because Sean believed it was. It didn't have the credentials of a Buddha's head or a crystal skull. It was just a passport photo of a girl, stuck to a small piece of card so she wouldn't bend. Easy for her to bend, rattling around in Sean's bag. In many ways, it would have been better to keep her in his wallet. But wallets, one was always hearing, weren't safe in Manila. Pickpockets, razors, guns, badges. Only two days ago, Sean had heard about a Japanese tourist held up by a couple of cops near Roxas Boulevard.

A face that would have launched a thousand ships? Probably

not, but that was okay. Dunkirk launched a thousand ships; launching a thousand ships was nothing to shout about. Enigmatic smile? No, and that was okay too. Enigmatic smiles were hype, good for nothing but messing with your head. This girl you could trust. Honest, solemn, especially in the eyes. Eyebrows, raised a little. Could have been about to ask a question, or to hear one answered.

Exhaling, Sean lay back across the carpet, resting the photo on his chest. He noticed the room was big enough so that – should you happen to be lying on the floor – the ceiling was about all you could see. A flat beige plane above, fading to darkness. A flat plane above, might be a plain below. A desert, with cracks as dried-up river beds.

Calm stole into Sean's solar plexus, radiating from the girl's point of contact. In five minutes, she'd be easing down his limbs, reaching up his neck. He came close to smiling. At this rate, sleep was on the cards. Seemed like a funny idea, having a nap when the *mestizo*'s Mercedes was weaving through the streets towards him.

Keeping pace with the girl's progress across his body, the desert fleshed itself out. Water marks were shadows on the dunes, blistered paint was scrubland. From the dunes to the scrublands, an indistinct line of dots made the tracks of a camel train. Were the remnants of the spider web a mirage, or was it the other way round? Sean was finding it increasingly hard to tell.

A waste, he reflected, all those Temazepams last night. Sat up for hours, frigging around with those weak little pills, when he could have been drifting over some corner of the Sahara. Crazy, not to have thought of it.

But forget last night. What about ten minutes ago?

Or was it fifteen?

Whatever. Ten, fifteen, he'd been a headless chicken. Punching the wall, freaking out. Sean had to smile. He could picture his expression when the phone had started ringing. Jaw dropping, pulse jumping.

All okay now, thanks to his charm, his beta-blocker angel.

One day, he hoped to meet the girl in person. He'd see her in a street or something, and he'd walk up and introduce himself. Tell her all about the tough times she'd helped him through. The way she had of relaxing him, coaxing him out of trouble. He'd thank her, very politely but also genuinely, with warmth and feeling. Then he'd say goodbye, and they'd go and live their separate lives.

Poignant. The day-dream could put a lump in his throat. Especially because it was a dream that would never come true. Sean didn't know the girl's name and address, or even her nationality. Since finding her, abandoned on the floor of a passport-photo booth in Le Havre harbour, clues had been thin on the ground.

Sean continued his aerial scan. Over to his right, a network of parched tributaries. Over to his left . . . What was that? A meteor crater?

Forcing his way out of his drowsiness, he managed to focus for a couple of seconds.

'Oh,' he murmured. It was a bullet hole. Well, no great shock. Unexpected menstruation had been clutching at straws, and shaving accident was plain stupid.

So the telephone torturer had shot upwards, maybe with the barrel under his chin or in his mouth. Then again: pistol, low velocity, lead bouncing around the bone, no guarantee the bullet's going to come out the other side, let alone keep its trajectory. So maybe the guy had missed the first time. Missed because he was nervous and an idiot, and he'd had to try again.

Probably the latter, Sean decided with a satisfied nod. That the guy was an idiot was a given. Obviously he'd been here for a meet: nobody could have checked into Patay for pleasure. So what did he need? Signposts? Hotel Patay was the hit hotel. It was written all over its bleeding sheets and empty rooms. If he hadn't seen it straight off, he was in the wrong line of . . .

The desert shimmered and disappeared. Sean sat up, the photo tumbling off his chest, forgotten. On the floor, half covered by dust and broken plasterboard, the steel plate coldly reflected the light of the bedside lamps.

'You,' he said, raising an accusing finger. 'Are all about me.'

The moon orbits the earth. High tides and low tides come and go, the cause being gravity but the reason being nothing. The moon might have been bigger, further away, closer. It just happened not to be.

There was no point in Sean asking himself why Don Pepe wanted him dead. Mundane as the moon, the question wasn't worth a second thought and barely worth the first. And anyway, even if he'd been inclined to ask, he'd have found there wasn't time. At the same moment he was pointing at the steel plate, a grey Mercedes was pulling up opposite the hotel. It was instantly recognizable in Patay's quiet cocoon; there weren't many engines in Manila that purred.

No fool, Don Pepe. Called to say he was coming late, then arrived early, catching the mark unawares. The car doors opened and closed. Four slams, four men. Even the driver was on his way up. Told, Sean speculated blankly, that there was no need to keep the motor running as this job could take a while.

Now, magically, the room was cold. A sauna transformed into an icebox with a jingle of car keys and a low murmur of conversation, floating up from the street outside.

5

Watched by the telephone, the dial its insect eye, Sean unconsciously traced the dead torturer's last movements. He hovered by the door for several seconds before remembering that Patay only had one staircase, one exit, and the men were already approaching the building. Next he wrenched pointlessly at the bars on the window, which would have dislocated his shoulder before shifting an inch. And finally he ended up in the bathroom, where he established that there would be no escape through the tiny air ducts.

The telephone made for an indifferent witness. But Sean's reflection in the bathroom mirror, making contact as he turned away from the vent, was less detached. Even under pressure, the sight was arresting.

His face seemed to be in a state of flux. Unable to resolve itself, like a cheap hologram or a bucket of snakes, the lips drew back while the jaw relaxed, the stare softened while the frown hardened. Fear, Sean thought distantly. Rare that one got to see what it actually looked like. Other people's, sure, but not your own. Intrigued, he leaned closer to the mirror, ignoring the footsteps that were already working their way up the stairs.

The Conquistador

I

'Aaaah, we're going to be late,' said Don Pepe, breaking the tense silence of the last five minutes.

Jojo nodded and nervously pushed his thumbs into the padding around the steering-wheel. 'Yes, sir, we are. I'm sorry.'

'The hotel, now this.'

Jojo paused a moment before saying 'Yes, sir' again. He was leaving time for Teroy to add his own apology. After all, he'd been the one who had suggested Hotel Patay in the first place. But Teroy, sitting in the passenger seat, wasn't saying a word. No sense diverting Don Pepe's irritation on to him, when he could keep his head down and his mouth shut and let Jojo take all the abuse. Fair enough. Jojo would have been doing the same thing if their roles had been reversed.

Clearing his throat, Don Pepe continued. 'Aaaah, interesting, Jojo, that you should have chosen to come through Quiapo, when you know how the road-works are holding everything up.'

'Yes, sir.'

'I suppose you thought that at this time of night the traffic would be light.'

'I did, sir.'

'But, eeeeh, now you can see that actually the traffic is quite heavy.'

'Yes.'

'Hired as a driver, and you don't know where the traffic will be heavy in Manila.'

'It was a bad decision, sir. Please accept my apologies. In future, I will remember to avoid Quiapo when the road-works are still unfinished, even at this time of night.'

In the rear-view mirror, Jojo saw Don Pepe reach into his breast pocket for his silver matchstick-dispenser. 'I would hope you would remember. I wouldn't want to have another evening like this.'

'No, sir.'

'Naturally I shall have to telephone Mister Sean to explain the situation, which will certainly be embarrassing. I don't yet know him well, but I expect that Mister Sean is the kind of man to be serious about punctuality. As a European, we can expect him to be serious about such things.'

Jojo glanced sideways and thought he saw Teroy roll his eyes.

'Perhaps I could call him for you, sir,' said a syrupy voice from the seat behind. Bubot had chosen his moment to speak up. 'If it were more convenient for you . . .'

'Convenient?' Don Pepe interrupted. The car held its breath while he sucked his matchstick. ' . . . Convenient to hide behind others, rather than accept responsibility for my mistakes?'

Bubot shut his mouth with an audible snap.

Jojo had been Don Pepe's driver for eighteen months. He had taken over from Uping, who'd been killed in the same botched kidnap attempt that had killed Bing-Bong, Don Pepe's over-weight and psychopathic nephew.

Eighteen months, and not once had a day gone by without Don Pepe making some kind of reference to Europe and Europeans.

Usually the reference would be subtle or banal. A passing comment on a change of political office in France or, noticing a tourist through the Mercedes' tinted windows, a remark on the endless variety of Caucasian hair colour. Nothing that, to a casual listener, would suggest anything close to an unnatural interest.

Unnatural only became clear when he turned to one particular subject. When, after time spent in his company, you realized that this was a man on a constant hair-trigger. One glimpse of the Fort Santiago ruins, the Intramuros walls, and he'd be off. Betraying himself with too much knowledge, too much passion and too much fluency. Out went the aahs and eehs and the long pauses.

'Pizarro took Peru with one hundred and eighty men. *One hundred and eighty men* against the Inca civilization! So on whose side, I ask you, must God have been fighting?'

'Naturally, you must understand that although Magellan was Portuguese, his service was to Spain.'

'Legazpi's only failure was Mindanao. And listen to me, calling Legazpi a failure. By 1571, Manila was in his hands.'

'Imagine, now, what it must have been for the Aztecs to see a horse. And not just any horse. A *war* horse, armour-plated with teeth like razors!'

'There are no churches in the Philippines. No houses of God, only huts. *Iglesia ni Christo?* It's an insult! In Spain there are churches. *Real* churches. Here, you only have huts.'

Here, you only have.

Here, *you* only have.

But neither Don Pepe's father nor grandfather had ever been to Spain. Don Pepe himself had been only once, in December of the previous year. Five days in Madrid, and two days in San Sebastián, the home town of his ancestors. The one thing Spanish about Don Pepe was his blood, and you only had to look at him to see that it was mixed. Not that anybody would ever dare mention it.

Nor, indeed, would anybody ever dare mention his trip to the motherland. Relentlessly discussed in the build-up to his departure, instantly taboo on his return. Taboo for no other reason than the expression on the old man's face when Jojo had picked him up from the Ninoy Aquino International Airport. He hadn't looked sad or disappointed, or even angry. He'd looked shell-shocked. For the next few weeks, the familiar lectures had been painfully muted. Omelettes rather than Cortés. Even now, half a year later, they still lacked their original length and vehemence.

'Mister Sean is British.'

Jojo, who had been lost in the blinking tail-lights of the jeepney in front, straightened in his seat and murmured, 'Yes, sir.'

'In 1762 the British occupied Manila, only returning it to our control with the 1763 Treaty of Paris. I'd imagine that most Spanish are a little ashamed that the British took their land from them, even if it was over two hundred years ago.'

'I suppose they are, sir.'

'But I'm not ashamed. The British were also great empire-builders. Personally, I respect the fact that they were strong enough to take the Philippines from us.' Don Pepe paused. 'And anyway, they only had it for a year or so.'

'A year is not long.'

'Of course it isn't. Next to four hundred years of Spanish rule, eeeeh, it's a mere bagatelle.'

Jojo and Teroy exchanged a glance. 'Bagatelle?' Teroy mouthed, and Jojo gave a fractional shrug. Don Pepe frequently lapsed in and out of foreign languages. Curiously, English more than any other.

'So,' Don Pepe continued. 'There you are. The British once occupied Manila. A little-known fact.'

Not in this car, it isn't, thought Jojo, and released the hand-brake, letting the Mercedes roll forward another couple of feet.

2

Bubot was the *sip-sip* king, all nods and smiles and feigned interest in the *mestizo*'s diatribes. Practically his job description. Not that Bubot was complaining – he'd wanted to be Don Pepe's right-hand man for as long as anyone could remember. The moment the news had come through of Bing-Bong's death, Bubot had been falling over backwards to catch the old man's eye. People said he'd have cut his balls off if he'd thought Don Pepe would be impressed. There had even been a rumour that the true purpose of the kidnap attempt had been to get Bing-Bong out of the way. Crazy rumour. Anyone who knew the *sip-sip* king also knew that he didn't have the wit for anything so elaborate.

The *sip-sip* king could keep the back seat. As far as Jojo and Teroy were concerned, the front seat was the place to be. They, at least, had their backs to their boss. Like kids in the corner of the class, they could let the teacher's voice fade to a background murmur. They could gaze at girls walking down the street and exchange sly winks. They could even have conversations. With plenty of time to practise, they had perfected the art of talking at a level that was audible between them but didn't carry beyond the leather headrests. And when conversation failed, perhaps suppressed by a sixth sense that Don Pepe was listening a little harder than usual, Teroy had his gun to polish – the shiniest pistol in Luzon – and Jojo had his jeepneys to study.

It was, Jojo often reflected, a mystery. The wildly customized minibuses chugged down every street of every barrio. Jeepneys were like the faces of your family or the feel of rubber sandals on your feet. Jeepneys were like the taste of *rice*. Who's aware of the taste of rice? But Jojo was aware of jeepneys.

The catalyst had been glass. Lack of glass in the windows of the jeepneys, and mirrored glass in the windows of the Mercedes.

For some reason, cruising through Quezon City one morning, this had occurred to Jojo, and it interested him. The fact that he was provided with a slide-show of lives in the shifting traffic, and that the people outside were provided with nothing by the Mercedes but their own reflections.

Only an observation, no great meaning, but it had been a hook. A slight tilt on an everyday sight, to make him look at the everyday sight through fresh eyes.

From that moment, Jojo's appreciation of public-transport vehicles grew from each traffic jam to the next. He began rating jeepneys from one to ten, based on anything from the quality of side-panel paintwork to general cleanliness and upkeep, and felt genuine pleasure when he saw a design worthy of an eight-plus.

The nameplates above the windshields had been one of the last revelations. Extraordinary that he could have known 'Dragon Punch Lady' ran the length of Edsa, or 'Future Shock' ran from Makati to Bicutan, but that he'd never wondered who the dragon punch lady might be, or what shock the future had in store. Extraordinary to live in a country that teemed with carefully thought-out messages, brightly emblazoned on huge plastic strips, that almost nobody ever bothered to read. Maybe this was why the owner of 'My Secret Lover' felt so confident about letting his secret out.

Like most things in Manila, it was after dark that the jeepneys came into their own. Their coloured lights were switched on, their fake chrome glowed dully under neon shop signs. Tonight, they looked to Jojo like miniature mobile nightclubs, packed with a tired and listless clientele. Or packed with bandits. Many of the passengers had tied handkerchiefs over their mouths to filter the exhaust fumes. Bandit commuters, lit by the soft red and green interior bulbs.

'Aaaah, phone,' said Don Pepe.

Bubot dived for it. The car phone, installed six weeks ago, sat within easy reach of Don Pepe's hands, and so far he hadn't picked it up once.

'I shall call Mister Sean now.'

Teroy coughed and half-turned in his seat. 'Actually I am not sure that Patay's lines are operational. If you remember, sir, it is why Jojo needed to hand-deliver your note to him this morning.'

'Of course I remember, Teroy. And I also remember explaining to Patay's manager that if the lines were not working by this evening, I would make my displeasure acutely known to him. The idea that Mister Sean would be without a working telephone . . . eeeh. What if his captain wished to call him? Imagine, he wouldn't be able to get through!'

Suck.

'Number.'

Teroy reached into his breast pocket and pulled out a card. '368–2266.'

'3 . . . 6 . . . 8 . . .'

'2266.'

'2 . . . 2 . . .'

'66.'

'6 . . . 6 . . .'

There was a pause.

'Aah. It is ringing.'

The car breathed a quiet sigh of relief.

Jojo tuned out Don Pepe's conversation with Mister Sean. He didn't like the way Don Pepe talked with Europeans. As stubborn and pushy as ever, but with a subtly ingratiating note that made Jojo feel curiously ashamed. The *mestizo* never talked to Filipinos that way.

Worst of all, the subtly ingratiating note was wasted. Don Pepe's European business acquaintances were all merchant seaman, a graceless bunch, whereas Filipinos invariably treated him politely. Even his enemies. Even the most earnest young lawyers, on the old man's back for one reason or another, hoping to make a name for themselves or to reach an early grave. They'd say '*po*' as they handed over a subpoena, hold open courtroom doors to let him pass. Unless Bubot had beaten them to it.

Always a shock, seeing a European being rude to Don Pepe. Once, Jojo and Teroy had been escorts to a meeting in which an Australian seaman, first mate of the *Mentalese*, hadn't been wearing a shirt. Not a stitch on his chest. Jojo hadn't known where to look. Teroy said later that he'd been in two minds whether to shoot the Australian or shoot himself.

Born loud and born rude, Jojo would have been forgiven for thinking, watching the pale faces stumbling in and out of Angeles bars. But there were exceptions to keep him with an open mind. Mister Sean, for example, was an exception. He'd been to the Philippines often enough to have picked up some good manners. Used '*po*' where necessary, and spoke Tagalog when he could.

Who had it right? Hard to say. Just about everyone deserved politeness, but sometimes Jojo felt a guilty envy when Europeans interrupted Don Pepe in mid-conversation or raised their voices at him, or better yet, clapped him on the back. An envy that faded as the *mestizo*'s eyes glazed and the vein in his temple thickened.

Reminded Jojo of a story his father had often told him, back when the family had lived on Negros. In the servants' quarters of Don Pepe's hacienda, squatting under the cool of the stone arches, chewing on the sugarcane his dad sneaked home from the plantation.

'Panding,' Jojo muttered, half-hearing his father's voice, 'was an orphan . . .'

3

Panding was an orphan. His mother died during childbirth, and six years later he lost his father, uncle and two aunts, trapped by an unusual bushfire during a long hot summer. With that sort of introduction to the world, no one was surprised that the orphan reached adulthood a little mad. Not very mad, only a little. Nothing you'd pick up in conversation or over a glass of home-brew. In fact, you'd only ever see it at one time: when he had a machete in his hand.

People in the fields called it a red mist. Look hard enough and many of them claimed you could see it, floating around his head like tobacco smoke or steam off the workers' backs in the early morning. Fat-Boy, overseer and whip-man, used to say that he set Panding on new crops the same way he set his dogs on monkeys that strayed too far from the tree-line. And just as no one would go near Fat-Boy's dogs when they had a monkey in their jaws, no one would go near Panding while the mist was in his head. A rule of common sense: watch at a distance.

Which meant nothing to Don Pepe. Firstly, Don Pepe didn't know the rule because he only ever saw his plantation from the balconies of his hacienda or from the saddle of his Portuguese horse. Secondly, even if he had known the rule, the idea of bowing to the madness of a cane cutter would have been as ridiculous as paying his workers' salaries during the six months that sugar was off-season, or not screwing their daughters.

The days after a light rainfall gave Don Pepe the chance to gallop his horse – something he would never do unless the soil had softened. In the Negros heat, the earth could bake as hard as rock, and even Portuguese-born horses could break a leg in those conditions.

That day, this day, his gallop took him to the hectares supervised by Fat-Boy. A rare visit, as these were the outer reaches of his estate. So it was as much out of surprise as duty that Fat-Boy's men stopped what they were doing, stopped stacking and slicing, and lowered their heads in the appropriate mark of respect.

'Fine day, sir,' said Fat-Boy as his boss approached.

'Eeeh,' said Don Pepe affably. The ride seemed to have put him in a good mood. 'It is. A fine day. God's touch apparent in all we see.'

The statement did not appear to need further comment, so Fat-Boy let the silence grow while the *mestizo* contentedly scanned his kingdom. Then both men's heads were turned by a sudden noise. A smack of a blade. Panding hadn't put his machete down.

'Why hasn't that man stopped work?' said Don Pepe, adjusting the brim of his sun-hat to see better.

Fat-Boy paused. Other overseers would have been quick to pull out their whip, using the ominous note in the master's voice as an opportunity to prove their ruthlessness. But Fat-Boy wasn't a cruel man and had no wish to see Panding unnecessarily punished, so he considered his answer carefully.

'I expect, sir,' he eventually replied, 'that Panding wants to show you how keen he is.'

'Keen,' Don Pepe said. 'That's good. But I think he is too keen. I think the other workers could see his keenness as a lack of respect. So, ah, make him stop.'

'Make him stop, sir?'

'Yes, stop.'

'Stop him, sir?' Fat-Boy repeated.

'Oh. Deafness.' Don Pepe pulled out his riding-crop and hit Fat-Boy across the side of the head. 'Is that better?'

' . . . Much better, sir.'

'Good. Now, are you going to stop him or not?'

'Sir, I . . .'

'Yes, or no.'

' . . . Yes, sir.'

Don Pepe sat back in his saddle expectantly.

It was a short distance to where Panding was cutting, but Fat-Boy made it seem long, walking slowly, eyes to the ground, shoulders slumped. Just as he was about to reach Panding, he turned around, shooting a quick glance at the onlookers, and then at Don Pepe. The *mestizo* wasn't even watching. His attention seemed to have been caught by the whitewashed walls of his hacienda, peering out of the jungle like a skull in tall grass . . .

'Like a skull in tall grass.'

Jojo blinked.

Moments ago, his father's voice had been in his ear and the image of the hacienda had been clear in his mind. He'd been hearing the low buzz of flies and the distant cracks and shouts of the plantation. And then, abruptly, it all slipped away.

He blinked again, frowned, exhaled slowly, and remembered.

This was the part of the story where he usually interrupted his father, breaking in with anxious sighs and questions. It had been 'Why didn't Fat-Boy run away?' when he was younger. And 'Why didn't Fat-Boy explain about the red mist?' when he was older. Eventually, he gave up asking the questions altogether. His father had no answers. Just a shrug and 'That was the way it was.' It made him sound like a priest.

From the seat behind, Don Pepe sucked his matchstick loudly and spat out a splinter of wood.

'Last year the hotel was, what, a very good hotel.'

He was still talking to Mister Sean.

'But now my associate tells me it is falling down already . . .'

An associate, no less. A pity Teroy's English was so limited, because he'd have been flattered to hear himself described as an associate. Jojo looked to his right, thinking he might tell him. A chance for one of their covert conversations while the *mestizo* was occupied. But Teroy was facing the other way, staring out of the passenger window, and for no good reason, Jojo was sure he could feel Bubot's eyes on the back of his head.

Slightly disconcerted, Jojo shifted position to obscure himself more fully behind the headrest.

Fat-Boy reached swinging distance of Panding's machete, and crossed himself. Then he lunged forwards.

'Fat-Boy is as crazy as Panding,' said one of the onlookers.

But Fat-Boy wasn't crazy. A barked order would have fallen on deaf ears, and the whip would have redirected the machete towards his neck. So instead he had moved to hold Panding, pinning his arms to his side in a fierce grip. Fat-Boy's only hope was to hang on until either the red mist passed or his own strength faded.

For two or three minutes, the two men stood in the cane, rocking slightly as Panding tried to break free. Then, finally, the tension began to ease out of their muscles. The moment of oddly motionless danger was over. Fat-Boy released his grip, and Panding's machete dropped straight from his hand.

'The boss,' said Fat-Boy breathlessly.

Panding looked dazed.

'He wanted you to stop.'

If Fat-Boy was over-confident when he returned to the *mestizo*, he could hardly have been blamed. He had faced death and lived to tell the tale. But Don Pepe was not impressed, and made a point of saying so.

'I'm not impressed with the way you control the workers,' he said.

Fat-Boy smiled. 'I control them the best I know how, sir.'

'Then perhaps you should learn more about how to control them. Learn from the other overseers.'

'Or the other overseers could learn from me.'

Don Pepe's eyes screwed up at this blunt reply. 'Oh?'

'My workers cut and stack faster than theirs, and I lose less of them.'

'Really.'

'Yes, sir. The less I lose, the more work gets done.'

'Is that so?'

'It is, sir. In fact, I believe that if the other overseers were to . . .'

'In other words,' Don Pepe broke in, 'just so that I can make this clear, you disapprove of the way I run my plantation.'

The coldness of the tone immediately returned Fat-Boy to his senses. 'Oh, no, sir!' he replied emphatically. 'I would never do that! I was only . . . I was . . .'

He hesitated, struggling to find the right words.

'You were only what?'

'It was that I . . .'

'Please go on.'

'I . . .'

'Mmm?'

'I . . .'

'Mmm?'

But Fat-Boy's mouth was failing him. He was confused. He couldn't comprehend how, in the space of a few minutes, he'd managed to find himself in such hazardous and unfamiliar waters. So, instead, made mute, he made a gesture. At different times to different people, the kind of gesture that might mean friendliness, affection, an introduction into conspiracy or emphasis during a debate. Or, in this instance, an appeal for help.

His hand, sticky with sweat and juice from the sugar, reached out to rest on the *mestizo*'s leg. He withdrew it immediately, in recognition of the mark he had overstepped, but immediately was too late. A print remained on the cream silk, proof of the act.

Don Pepe's white eyebrows shot up so fast and high that it looked as if they might shoot off the top of his head and fly away like seagulls.

'Aaah,' he gasped incredulously.

Fat-Boy's face flushed, blackening with horror.

'Eeeh . . . That man will do it. He seems good with a machete.'

'Sir, if I could buy you some new trousers. Several pairs, all silk, several colours and . . .'

'Don't be ridiculous. You couldn't possibly afford it.'

'I have savings that might be used for . . .'

'You seem to be missing the point. It isn't trousers, it's principle. You can't expect me to ignore principle. I know you understand that.'

'I understand, but . . .'

'Good. Now then . . .' Don Pepe beckoned to Panding with his riding-crop. 'You. Come over here. I can't spend all day over this.'

Fat-Boy stared blankly at his fingers. 'Sir, please, a moment. If I am cut now, I will die from bleeding. If you permit it, at least let them be cut off tonight. We can light a fire and heat an iron, and the wound can be properly sealed.'

'You're a physician?'

'Sir, please!' Fat-Boy's voice was breaking. 'I will not recover if my hands are cut off here.'

Don Pepe considered this for a few moments, tugging thoughtfully at the loose folds of skin under his chin.

'Very well. I shall not be able to watch because I have an engagement tonight. Aaah, dignitaries from abroad. But tomorrow,

I shall check on you. Oh, and if you try to escape, I'll feed your family to your own dogs.'

' . . . Yes, sir.'

The *mestizo* nodded. Then he wheeled his horse, dug in his spurs, and disappeared in a cloud of dust.

The next day, as promised, Don Pepe came to check up on Fat-Boy, who was convalescing in his hut, tended by his wife and Panding himself. The master took a brief look at the feverish, bloodied figure, and shook his head. 'Hands,' he said. 'I said hands. Not hand.'

Fat-Boy didn't survive the second amputation. Panding blamed himself. Three days later, he ran amok on people rather than crops, and was cornered in the cane.

But not killed.

Somewhere in the recesses of Jojo's childhood memories was an old man for whom errands were run. Eggs or water, carried to a house that sat separate from the others, on the edge of the *barangay*. A figure in its doorway, rarely out of the shadows, bent with age, vaguely frightening from a distance. Close up, quiet and reassuring. He ruffled your hair so weakly that it felt like a breeze, and he had soft dry skin that smelled of the split husks beneath coconut trees. And he was gone by the time Jojo was five or six.

'So . . . why did Don Pepe let Panding live?'

'Jesus, son! These questions you ask. That was the way it was!'

Don Pepe, old as any church that Jojo had ever seen, moved in mysterious ways.

4

Making good time, said the green LCD clock on the dashboard. Having cut through side-streets, slaloming past foot-deep pot-holes, they were going to arrive at Patay ahead of schedule. Jojo wasn't sure whether this was a good thing or a bad thing, in view of the fuss there had been over punctuality. Now that the meeting had been moved to a later time, which arrangement was the correct one to stick to? Which punctuality took precedent? Probably the original one, Jojo guessed, so he took no detours and stuck to the quick route.

On Sayang Avenue, just before the left to Sugat Drive, the Mercedes ran over a cat. It was caught by the headlights for a frozen second, then caught by the left front wheel. The impact shook the car and made everyone hunch their shoulders – except Teroy, who had never hunched his shoulders in his life.

' . . . Was that a dog?'

'It was a cat.'

'A kid?'

'Eh! Eh! We hit a kid?'

'I think it was a cat, sir.'

'Not a kid?'

'A cat, sir.' Jojo steered the car over to the side of the road. 'I'd better check the car for damage.'

'Hmm,' Don Pepe murmured, not yet sure whether this was something he ought to be getting angry about. 'Yes, you do that. You go and check.'

The tarmac was still half melted from the daytime heat. It sucked at the soles of Jojo's shoes as he walked around the front of the car, feeling along the bumper for dents, nicks or fur. Around the back of the car, the injured cat flipped and jerked in a pool of red light. At a guess, its back was broken. Jojo tried to avoid looking in that direction, but found he couldn't help it. His daughters kept a cat with similar markings. The cat slept at the foot of the younger girl's bed. There had been no mice in the kitchen for years.

'Damn,' Jojo said to himself. 'I can't leave it like that.' He walked to Teroy's window and motioned for him to wind it down.

'It's still alive.'

'Is it going to be okay?'

'No.'

Teroy rubbed his cheek. 'Run it over again?'

'We have to do something, but . . .'

'What's going on?' Don Pepe's voice snapped from the back seat.

'The cat is still alive, sir,' said Teroy. 'We're wondering what to do about it.'

'It's hurt?'

'Yes, sir.'

'Eeh . . . And is the car damaged?'

'No, sir.'

'Good.'

There was a pause, during which, in Jojo's peripheral vision, the twisting of the silhouette moved up a frantic gear. As the pause continued, Jojo realized that Don Pepe was waiting for him to get back in the car.

'Sir,' he said. 'Perhaps we should kill it.'

'Kill it?'

'Stop its suffering.'

'Ah. Ah, well, yes. Mercy, absolutely. Go on, then.'

'Right, sir.'

'Anyway, we're early for the meeting now, so there's no, eeh . . . no need for you to hurry.'

Jojo and Teroy glanced at each other.

'No need to hurry,' Jojo repeated warily.

'Yes. We're early now so you don't need to hurry.'

'Sorry, sir. You . . . want me to kill the cat slowly?'

A wrinkled face appeared over Teroy's shoulder. 'I beg your pardon?'

'Sorry, sir. I thought you were saying that –'

'Do you know, Jojo, if I have time tonight I shall say a prayer for your soul.'

'Kill it quickly, sir.'

'Yes, kill it quickly, sir! Kill it very quickly, sir! God in Heaven, what have I done to . . .' The sentence tailed off as the face retreated. 'Oh, just get on with it.'

Easier said than done. Jojo never used his gun. Come to that, he'd never used *any* gun. Age twelve, circumcision had come and gone, and age sixteen, he – and every other boy he'd grown up with – had lost his virginity to one of the three barrio whores. If only firing your first bullet was as straightforward as losing your virginity. Pay fifty pesos to a sharp-tongued but basically kindly lady, who showed you how to load a clip and squeeze on a trigger, and who didn't laugh when you got it wrong.

And now too much time had passed for him to joke with his colleagues about his inexperience with weapons, or even to mention it. Although in the back of his mind, he had a feeling that Teroy knew. Teroy had given him the automatic that was now strapped to the side of his chest, and when Jojo had outstretched his palm to accept it, his hand had dropped under the sudden weight and the pistol had nearly fallen to the floor. He hadn't expected the weight. Stupid, not to expect the weight of a big lump of metal, but there it was.

Four years ago. Four years since he had changed from being the son of an employee to an employee in his own right, and four years of worrying that one day his inexperience was going to be revealed. The real fear was that it would be at a moment when he was having to defend someone else's life. That seemed worse than if he were defending his own. A couple of nights he'd been unable to sleep, imagining the way he'd pull on the trigger, only to hear a hollow click from a hollow chamber. Teroy collapsing beside him as he fumbled with a safety-catch.

On one of those sleepless nights, his wife had come into their mouseless kitchen to find him sat at the table surrounded by bullets. He'd taken them out of the magazine so he could learn how to load and reload, but then had been unable to put them back in. His fingers had been trembling, and he was afraid that if he shook the bullets too hard they'd explode. So the two of them had stayed up together, fretting over the stiff spring of the magazine, loading and reloading until they were sure they'd got it right.

Well, Jojo reflected, now he was about to find out if they'd got it right. He reached for the holster under his jacket, tore away the Velcro and pulled out the pistol. It was as cold as a can of Coke, chilled by the air-con in the car.

Things to think about: safety-catch, recoil, two-handed grip, aiming, squeeze don't pull.

What a *loud* noise. Jojo might not have fired a gun before, but he'd often heard them, and they'd always sounded like popping. No louder than a firework, but oddly neater, more compact. But this – this was unbelievable. Ringing ears, blurred vision, dizziness, shock . . .

The cat was still alive.

Had he missed? It was certainly possible, given that his eyes had been closed for a good second or two before he fired. Should have been on the list of things to remember – keep your eyes open. *Idiot!* And he couldn't shoot again, because people in the car would want to know why he couldn't kill a half-dead cat with a gun that could shoot through walls.

But maybe he had hit it. Maybe it was mortally wounded – just a question of waiting a few moments more. The problem was, with the red from the Mercedes' tail-lights and the already matted fur, it was impossible to tell if there was a mortal wound or not. Jojo squatted down to see better.

With an epileptic spasm, the cat leapt up off the tarmac and on to his chest, where it clung with its claws and teeth. 'Oh,' said Jojo, and lost balance. He fell backwards and sat heavily on the road. The cat remained clinging. Instinctively, Jojo lifted his arms to make a cradle, held firmly enough to contain the animal's wriggling. It died in less than a minute.

Bubot and Don Pepe were engrossed in shop-talk when Jojo got back into the car, so they didn't notice the rips or the blood on his shirt. Teroy did notice, but being a good compadre, he didn't draw attention to it. '*Paré*, spare shirt in my bag,' he whispered, once Jojo had the engine running. 'In the boot. You can change when we go in for the meeting.'

'Thanks, *paré*,' Jojo whispered back.

Teroy smiled. Then, at a normal volume, he said, 'Let me have your gun. You can't reload it while you drive.'

Grateful, embarrassed, Jojo handed it over.

5

'Incredible,' muttered Don Pepe, looking through the car windows, shaking his head at the crumbling streets that led to Hotel Patay. 'Completely incredible. Teroy, what were you thinking of?'

'Mister Alain, sir. He once stayed here, so I thought . . .'

'Mister who?'

'Mister Sean's predecessor, sir,' Bubot chipped in. 'He was the first mate of the *Karaboujan*, until . . .'

'Oh, Mister Al*an*. "An" Teroy, not "ain" . . . Poor Mister Alan. He must have been very sad about the loss of his captain. Off Mindanao, wasn't it?'

'Palawan, sir.'

'Tch, tch. Thais, I dare say.'

Bubot cleared his throat. 'No, sir. Not Thais.'

'Cambodians?'

' . . . No.'

'Not us, surely?'

'Actually, sir, I believe it was.'

'Us? But I'd done business with him for years. *Surely* the *Karaboujan* has safe passage. Why on earth haven't you told me this before?'

'Sir, the *Karaboujan* was boarded on your orders.'

' . . . It was?'

'Yes, sir.'

'Eeeh.'

'You may remember, sir, the *Karaboujan*'s captain had been difficult with his payments for nearly nine months. We, you, felt he was getting too arrogant.'

'Ah . . . Ah, well, it's a bloody business, no question. Has to be.'

'You might say, sir, *nature of the beast*,' said Bubot, ambitiously, in faltering English that made Jojo wince.

But if the *mestizo* noticed the *sip-sip*, he didn't show it. 'Yes,' he said absently. 'It is indeed.' Then he gave a couple of long sucks on his matchstick. ' . . . So, eh, out of interest, what was the *Karaboujan*'s cargo?'

'Sugar, sir,' Bubot replied.

'Sugar? Was it really? And did we get a good price?'

'Very good, sir.'

Don Pepe smiled. 'Yes, of course we did. No Pepe would stand for anything less. Who took it? Seb?'

'Dante.'

'Dante. So there you are. A lesson for us all. Never lose your contacts, and never forget where you come from.'

'An excellent lesson, sir.'

'Almost makes me miss the sugar trade.'

'No one traded like the Pepes, sir.'

This time, Don Pepe did notice the *sip-sip*. '*Por favor*, Bubot,' he said languidly. 'Shut up.'

'Shut up,' Bubot echoed, absorbing the insult with an ease that came from long practice. 'At once, sir.'

Jojo leaned on the bonnet of the Mercedes, arms folded across his chest to hide the cat's blood, and shivered. He'd seen the hotel once before, that morning when he'd delivered the boss's note to the bruiser on reception. In daylight the building looked bad, a concrete corpse, but now it was something else. The single light on the second floor had reanimated it. Made it vaguely alive, it seemed to Jojo, or undead.

As the thought crossed his mind, Jojo heard Don Pepe say, 'All of us, I think, for this meeting.'

'Sir, don't you think I should stay with the car? This neighbourhood . . .'

'No. The purpose of this meeting is to put our business with Mr Sean on a formal basis. And the talk of the *Karaboujan*'s late captain has reminded me. I want to make a strong impression on Mister Sean, to make the impression last. For the sake of the *Karaboujan*'s new captain, if nothing else.'

Then, to Jojo's amazement, Don Pepe laughed. Or as close to a laugh as he ever managed. 'So, you see, I am expecting that the blood on your shirt will work to our advantage.'

Jojo let his arms drop to his sides.

'Aaah, heh, it will give the Englishman something to think about.'

'Yes, sir.'

Don Pepe gave another rasping chuckle and began walking towards the hotel entrance.

But Jojo paused before following. Just as the *mestizo* had turned his back, he thought he'd seen something appear at the single lit window. Two hands, fast-moving shadows, that looked as if they were pulling at the bars. And then they had disappeared, too quickly to be sure if he had imagined them or not.

'Jojo!' Teroy hissed, holding open Patay's frosted-glass door. Bubot and Don Pepe were already in the building. 'Come on! Let's go!'

The Squall

I

The bathroom mirror was gone, replaced by a buckled square of hardboard. And there were now hundreds of little Seans gazing up at him around his feet, and pooled in the plug-hole of the sink. 'Jesus,' Sean said, inhaling tightly. He checked his knuckles and felt around his forehead. There was no cut – a lucky break.

A lucky break from a broken mirror. Seven years' bad luck, with a lucky break.

That couldn't be right. He felt around his forehead again, not for wetness this time, just massaging his temples.

The glass crunched under his shoes as he took a step backwards. 'Think,' he whispered. 'Get a grip.'

Get a grip? He'd lost his face. There was no grip to get.

So instead he got his gun. And the spare magazine he'd put aside earlier, and the loose shells from his bag.

2

One of the men had blood all over his shirt. The same man whose hand, five times as big as his head through the spyhole's fish-eye lens, reached out and knocked on the door. It was Joe, Sean noticed with numb dismay. Of all people, Joe the driver.

*

The first time Alan had taken Sean to meet the *mestizo* was at a seafood restaurant on the waterfront, within walking distance of both the US embassy and the Manila Hotel.

The day had not started well. Alan was in a lousy mood because the captain had asked him to hold out for free safe passage on the next trip. A month earlier, the *Karaboujan* had lost money on a shipment of Malaysian latex. The cargo had been corrupted by the heat in the holds, and an insurance screw-up had left the *Karaboujan* accountable.

Sean, on the other hand, had his own worries. He'd heard plenty about Don Pepe. Plenty about the half-breed whose racket covered all shipping through Filipino waters. He knew his bedtime prayers, his ageless age, his matchstick and his power. But Alan, in a lousy mood, needed to take it out on someone, so he took it out by making Sean feel even worse.

'See that old man?' Alan had said as they walked across the docks.

'Old man?'

'Over there.'

Sean turned, saw crates, but nobody near them.

'You missed him.'

'Oh . . . Who was he?'

'Crazy man, worked cranes, been around the bay since I can recall. You want to know what he once did?'

'Sure,' Sean said, and looked around again. Squinting, he thought he could make out a figure in the shadows between the corrugated-metal containers, but it was early evening and the light was bad enough to play tricks.

'He chopped off the harbour-master's hands with a machete.'

' . . . Yeah?'

'Killed the guy in the process.'

'Jesus,' said Sean. 'Why did he do it?'

So Alan told him. A listless day on the seafront, a crazy docker, an over-confident harbour-master, a tyrant *mestizo*, and sticky fingerprints on a new suit.

At the restaurant, waiting for Don Pepe, Sean alternated between wiping his palms on his trousers and patting his breast pocket to feel the small square of his lucky charm.

'Quit wiping your fucking palms,' Alan had said, but Sean had ignored him. On the off chance that Don Pepe expected a handshake, he was going to be shaking the driest, unstickiest hands in Manila.

Don Pepe had not expected a handshake. When he and his entourage finally arrived, the *mestizo* didn't even glance in Sean's direction. Instead, he swept through the waiters who had appeared out of nowhere and indicated a couple of tables. In the time it took him to leisurely cross the restaurant floor, the tables had already been inspected, wiped and set.

Alan, Don Pepe, Bubot and Teroy all sat together. Joe and Sean, not so important, sat separately. Their job was to hang in the background while their respective bosses cut their deals. Neither man talked much. There was an awkwardness, partly at being strangers, partly at their shared status as small fry. They were also listening in on the next table's conversation. Alan pressing his point, and Don Pepe not giving an inch.

'Bery dippicult, bery unportunate. But it is not my problem.'

'All we're asking for is a single free passage. One free passage and we'll have covered the latex fuck-up. We can get business back to normal.'

'Eeh, business. You hab said the word that is on my, *ano*, mind. Nothing in this is ob a personal nature, Alan. It is business *lang*.'

'Then in business terms. The *Karaboujan* comes through here, what, six or seven times a year? If you don't give us passage, we're looking at bankruptcy. That means you're missing out on . . .'

'Do you know how many ships come through the Pilipino waters? What dipperence is one ship?'

'Exactly. So why not give us passage?'

'Heh, if you want to take your chances on the open seas . . .'

'We've co-operated for years, Don Pepe.'

'Yes, por years. So I think you know the way I work.'

Alan opened his mouth to say something, but changed his mind. He hadn't expected to talk the *mestizo* round.

'What can I say, Alan? This is lipe. *Mahirap buhay.*'

'Yeah,' said Alan tiredly. '*Talaga.*'

The edges of the *mestizo*'s lips curled upwards. '*Talaga?* Your Pilipino is improbing.'

'Improbing?'

'Getting, *ano*, better all the time. Ebery time we meet, better still.'

'Oh.'

'And, eh, what about your priend here? He can speak Tagalog?'

'Sean?'

'Yes,' said Don Pepe, turning in his seat, turning the shoulders of Teroy and Bubot with him as if the men were connected by thread. 'Mister Sean. Can you speak Tagalog?'

Sean stiffened. He had almost relaxed listening to the argument, and the sudden shift of attention had caught him by surprise.

'Eeh, can you eben speak English?'

'Yes, I can speak English,' Sean quickly replied. 'But not Filipino.'

'Not Pilipino.'

'*Hindi ba po.*'

Don Pepe's eyes lit up. '*Hindi ba? Hindi ba?* How can you say "*hindi ba*"? I say, can you speak Tagalog, and you say no . . . in Tagalog! So you can speak, *di ba?*'

'*Conté lang po.*'

'Aah! Only little, hah? Still, anyway, it's good you try.'

'. . . *Salamat po.*'

'Mmm. Bery good that you try,' the *mestizo* said again, sucked pensively, then he turned back to Alan. 'Okay, I hab changed my mind. I want Mister Sean to continue learning Pilipino, so the *Karaboujan* will not be bankrupted. But, *ano*, this time only.'

Alan's face screwed up in suspicion. 'You're giving us passage?'

'Yes.'

'Free passage?'

'Yes.'

'*Safe* passage?'

'Ob course.'

'Fuck me,' said Alan, features softening, shaking his head. 'San Miguels all round.'

Beer arrived for everyone except Teroy – who politely declined the bottle that Alan slid across the table – and ice was broken. Soon the other table was chatting, a surreal and good-natured conversation about the Federalization of Europe. Sean couldn't believe his ears. It was the very last thing he'd imagined he might hear at the meeting.

And with the other table chatting, it didn't seem right that Sean and Joe should continue sitting in silence. So Sean thought he ought to break some ice of his own, and introduced himself.

If in doubt, not least in the company of South China Sea pirates, err on the side of formality. 'I didn't ask your name,' he said. 'I'm Sean by the way.'

Joe nodded. 'Mister Sean, I am Joe.'

'Joe.'

'Yes.'

'Well, hi Joe.'

'Yes, hi.'

They exchanged smiles. Then Joe said, '*Mang* Don Pepe was bery happy with you, speaking our Pilipino language.'

'Seemed so.'

'But you know, Mister Sean, it was not the Pilipino language only. Really, it is because you already know to say "*po*". Por *mang* Don Pepe, that is good. But it is also good por me too.' Joe put his hand on his chest. 'As a Pilipino, por me it is good you use *po*.'

'Thanks. Uh, it was Alan. Alan taught me.'

'Yes, but . . .' Joe's voice lowered. 'Alan does not use *po*. You can excuse me, but I do not think Mister Alan is bery polite.'

'Sure I can excuse you,' said Sean readily. 'No problem.'

'Thank you.'

'My pleasure.'

'Yes.'

'So . . . want another drink?'

'No, thank you. One only, it's enough. I am dribing. Driber ob *mang* Don Pepe.'

'Then have something else.'

'Sopt drink?'

'Sopt as you like. How about a Coke?'

'Okay.'

'Okay.' Sean beamed. 'I'll get one in. My shout.'

3

'I wish you weren't the killer, Joe.'

Sweat oiled the area where Sean's forehead pressed against the door, making him slide against the wood. He had to make small readjustments to keep his eye level with the spyhole's tiny curve of glass. Sweat was also collecting in his hair-line, running either side of his ears, tickling his neck. Dealing with the itch was not a problem; a noiseless swipe would not have alerted the Filipinos to his close and watchful proximity. But he chose to let it stay, taking it as an opportunity to stay loosely in contact with his senses.

Strange, though. To think that even at a time like this, your skin could still get tickled. The mind intent and serious, and the body frigging around, letting you down. Like running from something bad, only to discover that your legs still ache and start to seize and you still get short of breath. Discovering that trouble doesn't provide miracle lungs, in the way you wish it would.

Sean relaxed his right hand around the grip on his automatic, then tightened it. The light caresses on his neck were starting to burn a little, and more itches were appearing elsewhere. On the small of his back, on the back of his thighs, his scalp, his wrists, his stomach. Each one kicking off another.

Sean wondered: is this what happens if you miss a scratch? Let an itch go, and suddenly you're dealing with an avalanche. Your whole life, fending off avalanches with a rub of the finger-nails here and there, unaware you're doing it.

An avalanche was far more in touch with his senses than he had planned, but it was too late to do anything about it now. Eliminate one and he'd have to eliminate the lot, and he couldn't afford to get so distracted, to lose what focus he had.

'Focus?' Sean whispered thickly. The tickling had infected his tongue. It had even, somehow, infected his vision and his hearing. Having covered the skin's surface it was working inwards, clouding him up with a needling crescendo, becoming abstract and ambitious.

'Can't manage much . . .'

Mouthed it, didn't say it. Or if he said it, he didn't hear it.

' . . . more of this.'

In the fish-eye, standing in the elastic corridor, Don Pepe

seemed to agree. Spitting out a splinter from his matchstick, he motioned at the closed door. Joe reached out and knocked for the second time.

The second time. The third time would be with the heel of a boot.

Time, then, to take the initiative.

And with that decision the itching had either consumed Sean entirely, or it had gone.

The suck of air from the opened door pulled another door shut, further down the corridor. Caught in the passing vacuum, the light bulb above the Filipinos began a single outwards swing. Their heads turned to trace the source of the unexpected slam. Sean, his gun already levelled, was unseen by any of them. Standing in the door-frame, as good as alone, a free agent in a split second.

The *mestizo* was photographed by the first muzzle-flash with his eyes half closed – the reactions of his blink half-way slower than a bullet. The second muzzle-flash pictured him falling backwards, still looking in the direction of the slam, his matchstick hovering in space an inch away from his lips. Teroy's head was already turning.

Sean pointed the gun at the next nearest figure. Third muzzle-flash: the *mestizo* was collapsing and the flop of Bubot's fringe had jumped upwards like an exclamation mark. Teroy, incredibly, had his pistol almost fully drawn. Joe hadn't moved out of profile.

Sean took a quick step back into his room, shooting twice more, these rounds aimless. The same movement, he spun around and shoved the door closed with his shoulder. Then he leapt forwards, landing heavily, face down on the floor.

There was no immediate hail of return fire, and no moans or screams from the shot men outside. When Sean lifted his head a few moments later, all he noticed was that the bedroom was full of blue smoke and the smell of sparks. Was it possible that he'd hit all four Filipinos? He couldn't recall the last ten seconds clearly enough to be sure.

4

The ship was high in the water with a light cargo of dried noodles and Levi jeans, and the salt spray still reached right up to the guard-rail. Beneath Sean's feet, the engine vibrated dully through the metal decks.

'Did I hit one?'

Alan shrugged.

'How do I know if I've hit one?'

'You don't have to know. You're only supposed to be getting used to the feel. So fire off a few more.'

Sean put easy pressure on the trigger, didn't jerk or yank, and nothing happened.

'Hammer,' said Alan impatiently. 'Remember. The hammer isn't back. First shot on this automatic won't do anything unless the hammer's back. First shot you have to cock it by sliding back the casing. After that, the recoil does it all for you.'

'Right.'

Sean tried again. This time his gun bucked and burst and ejected cartridges, and when it was over, he counted – four or five. Of the four or five white-tipped dorsal fins that had been following in the slop trail, four or five remained.

' . . . I'm probably missing them.'

'I said, it doesn't matter. You're only supposed to be getting used to the feel.'

'Well, I think I'm getting there.'

'Uh-uh. Not yet. You're still bunching up when you pull the trigger.'

'Oh.' Disappointed, Sean glanced down at the pistol in his palm. It felt as snug as a fat wallet, which, perhaps, was why it looked so unnatural there.

'Reload,' said Alan, and frowned when Sean hesitated.

'Something the matter?'

' . . . No.'

'You sure? If there is, fine. Plenty of crew could use the extra cash.'

'I was just wondering if I'd ever really need to use this.'

'One day it's going to be me captain of this tub, and it's going to be you dealing with Don Pepe alone. I wouldn't want to be doing that if I couldn't use a gun, so it's only fair that I make you ready. Not looking for anything on my conscience.' Alan pushed his peaked cap back on his head, then jabbed a stubby finger at the sharks. 'Now I want to see you blowing holes in those things. And no bunching up.'

'No bunching up. Okay.'

'So let's see it.'

Sean never did hit a white-tip, as far as he knew, and eventually he got bored with trying. Instead, he shot seagulls. Soaring, catching up-draughts, keeping pace with the *Karaboujan*, they made for almost stationary targets. And you could never kill enough to empty the skies around the crow's nest. There always seemed to be a similar number floating around, no matter how many had thudded on to the top deck or spiralled into the ocean.

5

When the return fire finally came, Sean had already crawled across the carpet and was behind the teak bed. The opening shot punched through the door, drilling into the brickwork between the windows. Then every inanimate object in the room burst into life. The burned telephone leapt off the bedside table, pillows shuddered and spat feathers, cupboards swung open, glass shattered, fist-sized chunks of ceiling vaporized.

But nothing was finding Sean. Curled on the floor with his arms over his head, there was no bullet with his name on it. And better yet, he had a plan of action. The very instant the shooting stopped or there was the faintest click of an empty chamber, he was going to be on his feet and covering the short sprint to the opposite wall. Aiming straight for the hole he'd clawed around the steel plate.

Seconds later, the click came. No nightmare, no treacle-syrup movement, nothing considered except objective and intention, leaving Sean with the mentality of a freight train. Unstoppable; anything in the way of a freight train would have to be insane.

This was in his way: crumbling plasterboard, peeling wallpaper façade, and a token structure of desiccated wooden slats. Asking to be obliterated, it gave way willingly.

Sean stumbled out of his room and into the next one along, just as the shooting restarted. Plaster grit was in his eyes and nose, in his hair and between his teeth. He spat, panted and blinked.

Then he saw that he hadn't stumbled into the next room along after all – he was in a corridor. A second corridor on this level of Patay, lined with windows on one side and doors on the other, apparently running parallel to the first. From the light cast through the hole behind him and moonshine from the street outside, he could see down most of its length. There were chairs lying on their sides, folded mattresses, scattered refuse, newspaper pages. And at regular intervals, the corridor seemed to be segmented by jagged ridges and short spikes. It looked like the inside of a vast backbone, a newly discovered fossil.

The guns stopped again. Their magazines were empty, or possibly the door had been blown open by the last fusillade, and the Filipinos were already moving cautiously inside.

Sean took a step forwards, then broke into a run. No sense in going forwards slowly, and certainly none in going backwards. Jumping over the segments and chairs, he registered other details. Under his feet, menthol-cigarette butts. Thousands of them, a year's worth of emptied ashtrays, white filters heaped and spread like cauterized maggots. Above his head, missing patches of ceiling through which a higher level of Patay could be glimpsed, darker and dustier.

As the end of the segmented passage grew nearer, Sean found a moment to think. He had to get out of this corridor and into the other. It was the other that led to the stairwell, and the only way out of the building. And, seeing as the two corridors ran parallel, all he needed to do was duck into one of the doorways he was passing.

He ducked into the next one. Ten or so feet to his right, the stairwell. Sixty feet to his left, under the still-swinging light bulb, Don Pepe and Bubot lay outside the entrance to his room.

'Two dead,' thought Sean. 'Two alive.'

He flew down the stairs. Flew, mid-air most of the way, his shoes making the barest touch on each step, just enough to control the descent.

Half way between Patay's first and ground floors, he heard the sound of Joe and Teroy coming down after him.

Son-Less

I

'Teroy, you are lucky that you are not a Japanese.'

Teroy looked puzzled. 'Lucky, sir?'

'Very lucky. If you were a Japanese, you would be dead now.'

' . . . Dead, sir?'

'Hara-kiri, Teroy. Suicide. Stabbed by your own sword, for shame that you made Mister Sean spend even five minutes in this cockroach-infested carcass of a hotel.'

'Sir, I can only apologize again.'

'My point is that you can do *more* than apologize. But I suppose it is a good thing that the Filipinos are not like the Japanese. If they committed suicide every time they made a mistake, there wouldn't be any of them left.'

'Very true, sir,' said Bubot.

'Eeh.' The *mestizo* sniffed reflectively. 'Jojo. Knock.'

Jojo knocked.

It was unusual that there was no movement to be heard from inside the room. After a knock, you might expect to hear a chair scrape backwards, or the sound of someone walking to open the door. Jojo glanced over his shoulder at Teroy to see if he had noticed the same thing, and he had. There was a slight frown on his forehead, and he was holding his gun-hand away from his body, a few inches from where it would naturally hang.

Seconds passed and still the door remained closed, with no sign of it opening.

Don Pepe gestured for Jojo to knock again. Behind him, Jojo heard Teroy exhale slowly.

Jojo heard the latch turn on the door in front of him, and as the door was yanked open, he felt the rush of air on his nose and lips. But the door slam – it came from the side, down the corridor. And it had been the kind of noise he had been waiting for, or expecting. So when it came, that was the direction he moved his head. To the side.

There was a hammer blow on his ears and a tight cone of sparks, etched into his vision even after his eyes had clamped shut. And an airless constriction in his chest, like a dive into the icy water of Don Pepe's indoor swimming-pool, air-con chilled.

Eeeh!

'You see, Jojo, in this tropical Asian climate, it is all but impossible to immerse yourself in cold water. But in Europe, daily immersion in cold water is not only possible, but a long-accepted aid to a healthy constitution.'

Eh.

'There are no churches in the Philippines. In Spain there are churches. Here, you only have . . .'

Ah.

'God in heaven, what have I done to . . .'

Suck.

'I said hands. Not hand.'

Old as any church that Jojo had ever seen.

'Jojo. Knock.'

The *mestizo*'s last words. That was the way it was.

2

Words filtered through the ringing in Jojo's ears.

'*Paré! Are you hit?*'

Jojo still had his head pointed towards the slammed door.

'*Are you shot?*'

Too dazed to know if he'd been shot or not, he didn't reply. He might have been shot. He didn't have the vaguest idea what had happened over the past few seconds, so anything was possible. And there was a strangely acute heat on the lower parts of his legs, around his shins and calves.

Jojo looked down and saw Bubot. The last time he had seen Bubot, he had been standing up. Now the *sip-sip* king had dropped to the floor and was lying like a Chinese beggar, knees folded neatly under the torso, face hidden, arms flopped out to catch spare change.

Bubot's head was pouring blood on to Jojo's trousers.

'*Move away from the fucking door!*' shouted Teroy.

But the only thing that moved was Jojo's eyes, flicking sideways to Don Pepe.

'*The door, paré!*'

Don Pepe was slumped with his legs splayed out in front of him and his body half twisted, one shoulder leaning against the wall, keeping him from keeling over. His chin and neck and shirt collar were bright red. The splashes around his nose were even redder. Pale skin, never in the sunlight, never out of cover except after nightfall. The whisper had it: *a touch of sun would turn him black in a day.*

'*The door!*'

Teroy grabbed Jojo by the arm and yanked him backwards.

'*He can shoot through!*'

' . . . He?'

'The . . .' Teroy broke off. Maybe it was to catch a breath. He was breathing heavily, almost panting, and glittering sweat-beads were forming over his face even as Jojo watched.

Mysteriously, Teroy started feeling around the belt-line of Jojo's trousers.

'Gun?'

'It's . . . it's in the car.' An odd panic slid into Jojo's gut. Familiar, after a second or two. This was his nightmare coming true: the moment he actually needed to use his gun, he was letting Teroy down. '*Kumpadre*, I left it . . . the glove compartment. I . . . didn't . . .'

'In the car,' repeated Teroy, anger flashing across his face. Then he nodded, wiped the sweat off his top lip, and reached somewhere inside his jacket. Pulled out a small revolver. 'Okay,' he said, flipping the safety-catch as he handed it over. 'It's okay.'

Jojo took the revolver silently.

'Now listen, *paré*. On three, we're going to shoot at the door. We're going to shoot at the door before he does. You use *all* the bullets. You *keep* shooting until all the bullets are gone.'

'Shoot into the room.'

'Into his room. On three.'

'Yes.'

'You're ready?'

'Yes.'

'You're sure?'

' . . . Yes.'

Teroy crossed himself with the barrel of his automatic. 'One.'

One, two, three. Noise, blood, Bubot begging for small change, Don Pepe sitting with his sunless skin and slick red jaw – these things were beyond understanding. But numbers emptied the mind, leaving room for other thoughts.

A single thought, as his thumb turned the wedding ring on his left hand.

Just past eight o'clock. Miranda would be working on her jigsaw. A big one, perhaps half a metre square when complete. He'd got home early the previous Saturday and found all the little pieces, scattered on the floor at the foot of their bed. Jojo had been surprised, and wondered why she'd bought it. Seeing her crouched over the box, studying the picture for clues, he'd had to ask himself: what would drive her to buy a jigsaw?

'Miranda,' he'd said anxiously. 'Am I neglecting you?'

She didn't look up. 'No.'

'Then why did you buy a jigsaw?'

'I didn't buy it. Nana Conché bought it for her grandson, but he didn't like it so she was disappointed. She threatened to throw it away. I thought that was a shame.'

'Oh.'

'I thought it might be fun to do.'

Yes, Jojo had reflected, I can see that, remembering the quiet and methodical way she'd worked out how to reload his magazine.

'I was afraid you'd think I was neglecting you. Since I've become the *mestizo*'s driver . . . working so many nights.'

Miranda still didn't look up. She'd found two pieces that matched. 'Well, that's why I thought the jigsaw might be fun. To pass time, waiting for you to get home.'

'Ah.'

'Why don't you help me do it?'

' . . . Okay.'

'Good. You'll see, there are so many pieces that it is really quite difficult. Probably too hard for Nana Conché's grandson. He would only have got frustrated.'

Jojo knelt beside her and started hunting for a bit with two straight edges. 'We should start with the corners. That's the way.'

Miranda tutted. 'I know. I've found them already. I have them here.'

'Ah, yes.'

' . . . There's dinner for you under the plate over there.'

'Have you eaten?'

'An hour ago.'

'Well . . .' Jojo shrugged. 'Let's just work on this.'

'One.'

His thumb turned the wedding ring.

'Two,' said Teroy.

Jojo left the ring alone, and gripped his gun with both hands. 'Three.'

3

Shoulder to shoulder with Teroy, eyes screwed up against the sparks and spinning chips of wood, Jojo had a bad feeling about his arms. They felt untrustworthy and oddly disconnected from the rest of his body. For the moment they were doing everything he asked – keeping level and as steady as the recoil would allow – but for the next moment, there were no guarantees. They seemed on the verge of rebellion, threatening to seize up and become useless.

It was as though they were aware of something he wasn't. If not for the convulsion of shock each time the pistol kicked, and the blankness that followed, he felt sure he'd know what the thing was.

No recoil. The chambers were empty. Teroy pulled him to

the side of the doorway. Then he grabbed the gun out of Jojo's hand, reloading it before he reloaded his own, sliding in the new bullets with the same unthinking confidence as a street conjuror rolling a coin between his knuckles.

Teroy said something, loudly, judging by the twist of his mouth. Wasted on Jojo, because directly after the word 'three', and the explosion of shooting, he had gone completely deaf. He couldn't even hear his own voice, shouting 'I can't hear you' back at Teroy, who seemed to be equally deaf.

The pistol was thrust back into Jojo's hands. Teroy had a finger in the air, and was staring hard at him with a look of urgency.

A second finger joined it. The peace sign.

Peace sign?

'*I can't hear you!*'

Third finger. Oh, thought Jojo numbly. It was starting again.

Again, Jojo had the feeling in his arms. But this time, despite the shock of the kickback, an image was starting to jell. Almost crystallizing in the gaps between the gunshots, splintering, then reconstructing itself. Each reconstruction a little quicker and more efficient than the last.

Green and blue.

Jungle around him, blue sky through it, and a clearing ahead.

In the clearing, an almost ordered scattering of slabs and boxes. A group of men in black suits, women with black parasols, centred around a building.

A large building for the provinces, though small for a city, doorless and windowless, whitewashed stone, ringed by an iron fence.

In this gap between the gunshots, hot sun on the back of Jojo's neck.

4

The Chinese mausoleums were spectacular. Huge and ornate, covered in flourishes and inlaid marble – as opposed to thigh-high boxes, rain-stained, with little inscription beyond a series of dates and names. But spectacular though they were, there was another that put them all to shame – Don Pepe's, the size of a small church, positioned in the very centre of the graveyard, surrounded by free-standing statues of chubby kids and the Blessed Virgin, and ringed by its own exclusive cast-iron fence.

Within the stone walls of the mausoleum, generation after generation of Don Pepe's family. Behind the fence, an army of ancestral spirits, seething in the still air around the tomb, peering out of the statues' eyes and impregnating the clipped grass under their feet.

Sweating in the tree-line that bordered the cemetery, along with the rest of his family and everyone else from the *barangay*. All of them invisible, Jojo guessed, to the cluster of élite mourners that stood by the mausoleum's gated entrance. Black-suited, stiff silhouettes around Don Pepe's coffin, apparently so grief-stricken that they were beyond screaming or crying.

Which was eerie. Jojo had never seen such a quiet funeral. And he wasn't the only one to find it uncomfortable, because when the priest had begun talking, somebody had let out a short wail, 'Ay-ay-ay' bursting out of a clump of ferns to Jojo's left. Probably Tata Turo's wife, judging not by the wail's startling loudness, but by the way it had ended. A muffled yelp as Tata Turo grabbed his wife by the throat and clamped his hand over her mouth – a noise that most in the *barangay* had heard before.

Jojo's mother sighed, shifted her weight from one leg to the other, and wiped at her face with a handkerchief. Her shirt, brilliantly white that morning, was now clinging to her back and stuck all over with leaves and small twigs.

He looked up at her, and she smiled.

'Are you okay?' she whispered.

Jojo nodded.

'Not too hot?'

'No.'

'Not too tired?'

'No.'

' . . . A little bit hungry?'

He thought for a moment. 'No. Really.'

'You're being very patient. The funeral is nearly over now. If you can hold out a short while longer . . .'

'Yes. I can.'

'Good boy,' she whispered, with the faintest note of surprise in her voice. Then she wiped the handkerchief over her face again. 'Good boy.'

A low amen drifted across the headstones, then rippled around the tree-line. The priest had finished his speech, and Don Pepe's coffin was being carried inside the mausoleum's doorway.

Suddenly, Jojo felt his father's hand in the small of his back, propelling him forwards. Not understanding, he dug his heels into the earth.

'Move forward,' his father hissed, and pushed harder.

' . . . Why?'

'Move forward!'

Jojo continued to resist. They had been hiding in the leaves for hours – since long before any of the élite mourners had even arrived. Over all that time, no one had spoken a word above a whisper, or made a movement any more violent than brushing away a fly. It made no sense to now burst out of that hiding-place, into the bright light.

'Why?' Jojo repeated, turning to his mother, appealing for help. But she had the same look of urgency as his father. She motioned with her arms.

'Go on, Jojo!'

'I'll be seen!'

'Yes!' said his father.

'Jojo! Do as you are told!'

'I'll be *seen*!'

'Yes! We want Don Pepe to see you!'

'Don *Pepe*?' Panic-stricken, Jojo looked back to the mausoleum. He caught a last glimpse of Don Pepe's coffin, just before it disappeared inside. 'But he's dead!'

'Dead?' said his father incredulously; then he had pushed a final time. Much too strong for Jojo to resist, at that age. Unable to do anything about it, he had stumbled out of the shelter of the bamboo sprays.

The sense of isolation and stark visibility was overwhelming. The sky was vast and cloudless. Dry grass crackled beneath his bare feet. The sun was hot on his neck.

Jojo's parents had been right. As the doors of the mausoleum had closed and the mourners turned to begin filing out of the graveyard, Don Pepe's head had inclined in his direction. No different from his hacienda, distinctive at any distance. Always recognizable by his erect posture and the rhythm of his stride, and – now – by his long black hair. And though Jojo couldn't see Don Pepe's eyes, that slight tilt of the head was enough. He knew the *mestizo* was looking straight at him.

Moments later, others had come out of the tree-line, but they had missed their chance. Jojo had been first. He was the only one to be noticed, and remembered.

5

Hair black, then grey, then black, then grey. Fat-Boy's hands and life, taken by a Kastila plantation owner with eyebrows as white as seagulls, cut by a young man with a red mist in his head. Panding, a stooped figure in a doorway, too frail to run errands for himself, in a grave by the time Jojo was five or six.

Don Pepe, always, but a *mestizo* only once. The last Don Pepe had probably never known his mother. Never married because he felt he never could. Maybe he reasoned: one more dilution and the blood will be gone. A desperate trip to the mother country, already too old and too late.

'Here,' he would spit from the back seat of the Mercedes, 'you only have . . .'

Here, you only have Filipinos.

'The *mestizo* had no son.'

Jojo repeated it several times. The only ears that might have heard him were deaf or dead, but the words were worth saying all the same, to feel the speech vibrate in his throat and to know his tongue had formed the sounds.

'He's dead.'

Meanwhile, Teroy reloaded their guns again. He was also mouthing. Probably curses and promises; what he'd do to the sailor for shooting his boss; what he'd do if the sailor was unlucky enough to be still alive.

'*Paré*,' Jojo said as his pistol was thrust back at him. 'We don't have to do anything to the sailor . . . I think we should . . . could just . . .'

Teroy kicked open the bullet-riddled remains of Mister Sean's bedroom door.

' . . . leave.'

Then Jojo was standing alone in the corridor, staring at the smoke and dust his *kumpadre* had disappeared into.

In turn, the *mestizo* stared at Jojo, his eyes not quite as sightless as his driver and bodyguard had assumed. He was beyond movement, and beyond much in the way of thought, but he had an idea of what had happened to him over the last few minutes. He was also, through blurred and blackened vision, still able to see.

See Jojo hesitate before following Teroy.

Dimly sensing what the hesitation meant, the *mestizo* felt angry. An indignant command rose inside him, but lacking the strength to burst through the bubble of blood on his lips, it remained contained.

Or – perhaps not. Perhaps his power was in some way surviving him. Because a few seconds later, his driver slipped through the Englishman's doorway.

6

The Englishman's room had been shot to pieces. He had escaped by smashing through a wall, then he had run down the line of rooms that ran parallel to the corridor. These rooms had had their own walls smashed out – for no clear reason besides Patay's internal collapse – leaving a broad segmented passage that, to Jojo, looked oddly like a backbone.

At the far end of the passage, Mister Sean was visible for a brief moment before he turned back into the corridor. Teroy wasted no time giving chase. Jojo was a footstep behind. Loyalty to the seething air around Don Pepe's mausoleum, or to his bodyguard friend. But committed, now, either way.

A Running Man

The stretch of wasteground opposite Patay was illuminated by refuse fires and the moon, glowing through a methane haze. Behind him, Sean could hear his pursuers, firing their pistols, stumbling over the same rubble that he had been stumbling over less than two minutes before. He could also hear the screams of a dying man in Patay's lobby. Rather than take the chance that the shaven-headed concierge would try to block his path, Sean had shot him.

Over the wasteground, he took random lefts and rights into narrow slum alleyways and side-streets. This, Sean had known, would be his only chance. Alejandro Street, Sugat, Sakit, Sayang, no chance. Too broad and open – alleyways and side-streets would be his salvation. And baptism, in an open sewer, covered by loosely laid boards.

Incredible, Sean thought, as he lost his footing and slipped into the metre-deep liquid trench. *Incredible*. It shouldn't be like this. At such moments, one should be as sure-footed as was necessary, just as one shouldn't have to worry about itches. Adrenaline *should* provide.

The bottom of the trench was like greased glass, and as soon as his shoes found it he slipped again. For a blind second, he was fully submerged. Then he was on his knees, hands and elbows gripping either side of the sewer.

'Fuck,' said Sean, after he'd wiped the shit from his eyes.

Two figures were standing a few feet away – Joe and Teroy. They'd kept equal pace through the lefts and rights, and now they'd caught up. He was dead.

But a heartbeat later, he was still alive. So – not Joe and Teroy, because he'd have been killed already, or at least wounded. And, after another wipe, he saw that the figures were much too small to be men. They were boys. Two street kids, watching him with startled and serious faces.

A clatter of boards snapped Sean back into action. This *was* Joe and Teroy, and they were close. In the same alley.

Sean hauled himself up and out.

More lefts and rights, and he still hadn't lost them. A couple of times he thought he had, and both times he'd been wrong. He'd slowed down to catch some breath and think about his bearings, and heard them immediately, hot on his trail. Near to vomiting with exhaustion, Sean had been forced to start moving again. Not running any more, because he couldn't, even to save his life. Clumsy, stealthless, moving was the best he could do. But at least Joe and Teroy were as tired as he was, because they didn't appear to be gaining.

And this had been going on for some time now, long enough to leave the slums and enter a new neighbourhood. Middle class – streets only slightly wider, but lined with individual houses rather than a mesh of shacks. Not so much corrugated iron. More greenery by the roadside. Would have been pretty in the late afternoon, a low orange sun catching the blossom that spilled over the fences.

A lot of blossom around. So much that it wasn't just on the trees and strewn over the tarmac. It was in the air.

2—I

Black Dog is Coming

I

The view outside the kitchen window was full of colour. Tarmac still blue and grass still green, even though the sun was almost behind the horizon and the sky was red. Anywhere else in the city, a red sky would have washed out the colours like a sodium lamp, but not here. This was a good neighbourhood, with separated houses and broad clean streets, and colour that could survive the loss of light for longer than seemed natural.

'Blossom,' said Rosa, brushing at the soapsuds on her wrists. It had hit the trees on Adonis Avenue last week, bursting over the fences like a snapshot of a waterfall.

'Clean,' she added a few moments later – a reminder to herself that the plates in the sink were as clean as they were ever going to get. Absently turned and wiped in the cool sink-water for the last ten minutes, the last dried rice-grain had given up its grip on the china some time ago.

In fact, a double reminder. The plates were clean but the kids weren't, and ideally she wanted them bathed and in bed – if not asleep – before her husband arrived home. Rosa pulled the plug, and watched her handsome reflection until the whirlpool sucked it down. Still a few years to go until she inherited her mother's white, rather than silver, hair.

Raphael, six, and Lita, eight. Raphael – fuzzy school crew-cut, round face, big serious eyes, and eyebrows that dipped in the

71

middle. Even when he was smiling, his eyebrows left him with a slight cautious frown. Lita – eyebrows exactly the other way round. Upturned, so that even when she was sad she looked like she might be about to break into a surprised laugh. An exceptionally pretty little girl, as her grandmother Corazon liked to point out – probably too often for Lita's own good. If Lita was going to turn out as beautiful as it seemed she might, the less she knew about it the better. At present, she appeared perplexingly unaware of her ability to manipulate anyone over the age of thirteen, and Rosa hoped she would stay that way.

Better to show her admiration and affection for her children with a hand through their wet hair and a thumb rubbed over their foreheads to clear a stray rivulet of shampoo, running too close to their eyes.

'How's the water?' asked Rosa.

Lita nodded. 'Good. Not too hot.'

'No,' Raphael agreed. 'Not too hot. Even when we climbed in, it wasn't too hot.'

'I notice you haven't asked for your duck.'

'Hmm.'

' . . . Would you like it?'

'Well.' Raphael shrugged. 'Okay.'

'Only okay? Not so long ago you wouldn't take a bath without it.'

'Yes. That's true. I would like the duck, please.'

Rosa handed him the yellow toy and he dropped it between his crossed legs. Almost immediately it toppled over on its side, then began to sink. The two halves of the plastic mould had gradually split at the base, releasing the sand ballast in small quantities each bathtime. For a few months, grazing your back as you lay down in the tub had become such a feature of family life that Rosa almost missed it when all the sand had gone.

'So,' said Lita. 'How was it at the hospital, Mother?'

'Oh . . . fine.'

'Did you save anyone's life?'

Rosa shook her head. 'Not today, Lita, no.'

Lita was disappointed. The previous month, Corazon had taken the kids to collect their mother from work. They had entered the hospital via the emergency ward, arriving at the same time as a number of casualties from a bad jeepney accident on Edsa. Fatalities had been lying on the floor, and there had been a lot of blood. Thankfully they were both level-headed kids, and unlike for their grandmother, no nightmares or sleepless nights had followed. But the incident had left Lita with a profoundly inaccurate understanding of her mother's day-to-day work, which Rosa's patient explanations failed to redress.

'Are you *sure* you didn't save any lives?'

'Quite sure. Though I did diagnose a case of appendicitis.'

'Appendicitis,' said Lita, brightening. 'Can it kill you?'

'Only in the hands of an incompetent doctor.'

'Incompetent?'

'A bad doctor.'

'Like Eduardo.'

' . . . Where did you get the idea that Eduardo was a bad doctor?'

'You.'

'Really?'

'I heard you say it to Dad last week.'

'Ah. Well, you have big ears,' said Rosa, and pinched them. Lita giggled. 'What about you, anyway? Tell me about school. Save any lives there?'

But Lita didn't answer. She was distracted by something her brother was doing.

Rosa turned around. Raphael had picked up the duck and was holding the split over his face, squeezing a soapy water-fountain over his mouth and chin.

'Are you drinking that, Raffy?'

'A little,' he spluttered.

'I've told you, the bath water is not the same as the drinking water from the kitchen tap. It isn't clean.'

'Of course it's clean! We've just had a bath in it! Look at all this soap floating around!'

'No,' said Rosa firmly, pulling the crushed duck from his fingers. 'It is not clean. But you are, so come on out, both of you. Let's get you dried off and into bed.'

2

Rosa watched Raphael slip into his bedtime shorts, holding out a T-shirt for him. She wished she could hold it in one hand, casually, by her side – but she couldn't. It had to be both hands. She also wished she didn't have to hold it at all – but she didn't feel she had a choice. The T-shirt had to be there, anonymous and available, should he want to wear it. Sometimes he did, when the weather and nights were cooler. Rosa preferred the cooler months.

The irony was that his sister Lita always wore a T-shirt to bed. She was aware, even if she didn't *know* she was aware, that it was proper to cover her as-yet-unformed chest. Lita hid her unformed chest, and Raphael didn't hide the chest that would never be formed. Moreover, Lita didn't need to hide her chest, whereas Raphael . . .

'Raphael doesn't need to either,' Rosa muttered to herself, and he looked up.

'I don't need to what?'

'Nothing,' replied Rosa, through a yawn she engineered unconsciously. ' . . . You want this T-shirt?'

Raphael unflipped a twist on the elasticated waistband of his shorts. 'No.'

'You sure?' said Rosa, and immediately answered herself, 'No. Okay. Fine.'

'We'll go and say good-night to Grandma,' said Lita.

'Yes,' said Raphael.

'Yes,' said Rosa. And that was the whole point. Rosa couldn't have cared less what Raphael wore to bed, once he was *in* bed. But every evening, last thing before being tucked in, the kids would go and say good-night to Corazon.

Rosa sighed. Then she folded the T-shirt and lay it back in the cupboard where, in any normal family with any normal grandmother, it would have belonged.

Corazon sat on the sofa, her interrupted book by her side. Lita sat on her lap, and Raphael stood with his arms clinging to her knee. Rosa stood in the living-room doorway, leaning against the frame, feeling blank and hoping to stay that way.

'Do you know what I was thinking today?' said Corazon.

'Uh-uh,' said Lita. Raphael didn't bother to answer, because he knew where the question was directed, but he tried to pull himself higher up his grandmother's knee.

Corazon brushed her fingers through Lita's still-damp hair. 'I was thinking what we will be able to do with this in a few years' time. Really, so many options we'll have. And so much fun, deciding the different ways you will wear it. We'll look at magazines together, and choose only the best styles.'

'Hmm,' said Lita. 'Actually, it isn't long enough for many different styles.' She pulled her fringe to the side. 'You see, I can put it to the side like this, or to the other side, but . . .'

'Ah, well.' Corazon lowered her voice to a stage whisper. 'Perhaps in a few years' time, your mother will stop cutting it so short.' Then she laughed. 'Such *beautiful* hair. I can imagine it long and silky, hanging to your waist. Or we could tie it back with a band, and maybe put a flower in there. Of course . . .' back to the stage whisper ' . . . only the prettiest girls can get away with wearing a flower.'

Lita looked thoughtful. 'I'm not *sure* I'd want to wear a flower.'

'We'll see! We'll see if you want to wear a flower, when you want to start catching boys! But listen to me. I can tell you, my angel, you will be catching boys even with no flower at all. You will be the flower!'

'Flower . . .'

'Yes,' said Corazon. 'Flower. In the sweetest way, you will break hearts.'

'And what about me?' Raphael chipped in, frustrated, unable to contain himself any longer. 'Am *I* going to break hearts, *Lola*?'

Rosa closed her eyes. It was the only way she would be able to avoid seeing Corazon's expression. If her eyes were open, she would have to look.

A thin smile, the measure of Corazon's genuine affection for the boy as it tried to break through the suddenly dead mask of her face. A perfunctory stroke of Raphael's cheek. A helpless glance at his bare torso.

'Of course you will break hearts, darling. Many. You will be a playboy.'

'I'll be a playboy, and Lita will break hearts.'

'Yes.'

'And we'll both be rich.'

'I hope so.'

'Good. We'll both be rich, with fantastically big houses. And I'll be a playboy basketball player.'

Corazon coughed. ' . . . A basketball player, darling?'

'Yes, a basketball player. I'm fairly sure. I've been thinking about it, and I think I'd be good.'

'Well, well. That certainly is a very nice idea. But darling, what about being something grander, like a lawyer. After all, basketball players need to be . . .'

'Right!' interrupted Rosa, opening her eyes with a snap. 'Bedtime.'

Refusing to meet Corazon's gaze, Rosa clapped her hands, and pre-empted the inevitable protest.

'Daddy's going to be late home from work tonight, so you can't wait up for him. So come on. No complaints.'

There were none. The brother and sister kissed their grand-mother and padded out of the room. Good kids.

3

It wasn't going to be too long before the kids outgrew their small bedroom. Come to that, it wasn't going to be too long before they needed separate bedrooms. Which was a problem, because there were only three bedrooms to divide up – two adjoining, and one at the far end of the house.

Corazon's was at the far end, and it was the largest. When she'd moved in, she had asked to swap with one of the smaller rooms, but Rosa had insisted she stay put, despite her husband's grumbles. At the time, there had been an unformed thought in the back of Rosa's mind – that by the time the kids needed their own space, perhaps Corazon would have passed on. In more recent years, particularly since the troubles with Raphael, the thought was still buried but had clarified itself a little.

'Open,' said Lita.

'Closed,' said Raphael.

'Open!'

'Closed!'

Rosa frowned. 'It can't be both open and closed. Raphael, why can't it be open? You'll boil like a couple of eggs if I leave it closed.'

'It *can't* be open. There's a hole in the mosquito netting. The mosquitoes fly in and get me.'

'Well . . . your sister doesn't seem to mind.'

'I know she doesn't! The mosquitoes don't get *her*. They leave her alone.'

' . . . That's a mosquito's compliment. They bite you because you taste so sweet.'

'No. They bite me because I sleep beside the window, but mainly because I don't drink beer.'

'Beer?' said Lita, and sat up in bed.

'Lie back down, honey.'

'If I drank beer,' Raphael continued airily, and also sat up, 'they'd leave me alone too.'

'I do not drink *beer*!'

'Of course you do. You sneak it from the fridge. It's completely obvious.'

'I do *not*!'

'Then why don't the mosquitoes bite you? Everybody knows that if you drink beer, you don't get bitten by . . .'

'They bite you,' interrupted Lita, 'because of the smell when you wet the bed.'

'Wet the bed?' Raphael threw his arms up into the air. 'That's the stupidest thing I ever heard! I haven't wet the bed for months!'

'You wet the bed last week.'

'What!'

'Every night, actually.'

'How would you know? With all that San Miguel, you're too drunk to remember!'

78

'I do *not* drink *beer*!'

'Enough!' said Rosa. 'Raffy, Lita does not drink beer. Lita, Raffy has stopped wetting the bed. Now, lie back down and show me this hole in the netting.'

Raphael sunk back on his pillow. 'It's up there.'

'Here?'

'Higher.'

'Oh. Yes, I see it . . . So how did this happen?' Rosa winced. 'No, on second thoughts, I don't want to know.'

'It was Raffy.'

'Lita did it with a knife.'

Lita's eyes bulged. 'A *knife*?'

'When she was reeling around one night.'

'Irrelevant. I said I didn't want to know. Okay, how about I cover the hole up with a bit of newspaper, and then you can sleep with the window open.'

'Hmm,' said Raffy. 'Yes, that's a good idea. As long as the newspaper doesn't blow away.'

'Well, sweetheart . . .' Rosa rubbed a hand on the back of her sweat-slicked neck. 'I don't think there's much chance of that tonight. There hasn't been a breeze through Manila for days.'

4

Rosa padded down the stairs. In the hallway, passing the living room, she nodded gratefully at the sound of the television, and walked briskly past the open doorway, eyes forward. Then she continued down the hallway, giving a thumbs-up to the slightly frayed Christ on their Last Supper wall hanging, and went into the kitchen. She planned to read the *Manila Times* over a cup of black coffee, maybe complemented by some Magnolia halo-halo-flavour ice-cream.

Corazon was standing by the sink, busily rearranging the clean dishes that Rosa had stacked half an hour before.

'Dearest,' said Corazon. 'I've been telling you since you were Lita's age. If you don't pile the dishes in order of size, they'll get chipped.'

'Because he doesn't want to be a *fucking* lawyer! He wants to be a *basketball* player!'

Corazon chose to ignore the bad language. 'Rosa, he is never *going* to be a basketball player. You know it, his father knows it, and I know it. Why let him dream of something he can never have? It's nothing but cruelty.'

'He's *six* years old! Two weeks ago he wanted to be an astronaut until you managed to talk him out of it!'

'An astronaut was unrealistic. Astronauts need to be in peak physical condition. A lawyer is realistic.'

'But right now he doesn't *want* to be a lawyer, he *wants* to be a basketball player! And who knows, by the time he's *seven* he might have completely changed his mind!'

Corazon sniffed. 'I don't believe I brought you up to use that tone of voice with me.'

'You didn't bring me up to be a doctor either,' snapped Rosa.

'Excuse me?'

' . . . Nothing.'

'What did you say?'

'I didn't say anything.'

'I distinctly heard you say something about the way I brought you up.'

Rosa exhaled. 'I said, you didn't bring me up to be a doctor.'

'Well, what a thing to say! May I ask you, who paid for you to go through college?'

'Uncle Rey.'

'Yes! And who had to go to Uncle Rey, *four* times a year, asking for yet more money?'

'Yes! And *why* did it suddenly become so important to put me through college? *Why* was it suddenly so important to get me out of barrio Sarap?'

'So, you would rather have stayed in Sarap?'

'I would rather have had a choice.'

Corazon let out a short, vicious laugh. 'A choice in barrio Sarap! That's a fine thing to say. A choice between being the wife of a sawmill labourer or the wife of a fisherman. Oh, the choices I had!'

'Right! The choices *you* had!'

'They weren't *choices*!'

'You had *choices* between men!'

'My God,' said Corazon, and crossed herself. 'You understand so little. You are a trained doctor in a Manilan hospital, and you understand nothing.'

'Jesus,' said Rosa, and didn't cross herself. 'Can we stick to the point? Can we agree that if a six-year-old wants to be a . . .'

What was it with the street-side blossom? The sun was gone now, burned away during the kids' bathtime, but Rosa was sure she could still make out the greens and reds and blues. What was it with the colours that made them so durable?

'I'm going to watch TV,' said Corazon. 'The hospital programme, it's on tonight.' Her voice was stiff and hurt, but somewhere in it was a softness. The same softness that lay in her expression when she'd talked to Raffy earlier, smile struggling with her dead face.

'*ER*,' said Rosa, without turning from the window. 'I'll . . .'

Corazon's footsteps hesitated.

' . . . come in later.'

'Don't be too long. The hospital programme starts in half an hour. You know I can't watch it without you, or I don't understand what's going on.'

'Half an hour . . .'

Rosa's mother left the room.

It came as a surprise. The headlamp flare on the road, everything etched into a sudden bright monochrome, with quick sliding shadows. A Mercedes with blacked-out windows, fast-moving.

A few seconds and it had passed.

Flower Power

I

Barrio Sarap was as unlike Manila as a shark to a milkfish. Separated from the capital city by one hundred miles and the Sierra Madre mountains, the barrio sat on the eastern coastline of Luzon, gazing over the Philippine rather than the South China Sea. The only stone building was the church. Outside of the lumber yard, which had its own private generator, there was no electricity. There were no phone lines. There was no tarmac. There was only one tapped fresh-water source, not counting the granite-filtered streams that ran down from the boondocks.

A hard rural life, but a resolutely siesta atmosphere – even the thud of a fisherman's home-made dynamite or a metal screech from the sawmill seemed distant and unobtrusive. The only real disturbances in the barrio were occasional alcohol-fuelled brawls and the late summer typhoons, which would rip though the nipa huts, turn coconuts into cannon balls, and bring high tides that could suck palm trees down in their wake.

Unless, as a disturbance, one counted the kind of dramas that unfolded around adolescence, and adolescent preoccupations.

Pre-marital sex meant – have sex, and you get married. Sex without marriage didn't happen. Frustrated Sarap boys were forced to collect themselves together into groups of threes or fours and make a trip into the mainland, where the girls were less stubbornly virginal. There they would head for the larger towns, prowl, and hope that their long and exhausting journey would be rewarded. That failing, they'd pool their money and hire a prostitute.

As for the boys from the mainland, they stayed where they were. No need to make the trip across the mountains. They knew that the coastline girls were provincial and conservative and didn't put out without a cast-iron commitment.

This was the power of the Sarap girls. In their own way, Sarap boys shared the same provincial values, and were damned if they were going to end up marrying someone who'd already been laid. So, where a future was concerned, Sarap girls were the only option. Their power: a smile was a good reason for a boy to wait on a hot dusty road, hoping the smile might walk that way again; an indifferent turn of the head was an agony of rejection – and both could cause sleepless nights.

Sixteen years old, knee-length cotton dress with a sun-bleached floral pattern, school-books under her arm. Rosa had silk hair that dropped to her shoulder-blades and skin that was as deep in colour as the sky. One day, a suitor would tell her that her beauty was as rare as her fingerprint, just before she rejected him.

2

Her house was about two miles down the coastline from her school in Infanta, the nearest town. Making the journey home on cloudless afternoons, she'd walk along the road. It was longer than walking along the beach – the road meandered inland at some points, through hamlets and paddy-fields – but most of the route was shaded by roadside palm trees. In the mornings, however, Rosa always followed the beach. At seven a.m., the sun was too low in the sky to be any bother.

A boy said 'Look' as she passed him. He was kneeling down a short distance away, with his back to her, beside two metres of fine netting to trap the milkfish fry that swam in the shallows. In front of him was the white plastic container in which he kept his catch.

Rosa stopped, a little surprised.

It wasn't until he had glanced over his shoulder, to check if she had heard him, that she recognized the boy as Lito. They were the same age and lived in neighbouring *barangays*, so Rosa was vaguely aware of his existence, but they had never exchanged words. He didn't go to school, and they had no friends in common. The closest they had come to a conversation was at a fiesta, when Lito's older cousin had asked Rosa for a dance. Lito had been his shadow, back-up in the background. When she had politely declined, Lito stepped forward to stand beside his cousin, and opened his mouth as if he meant to say something. But instead he'd nodded, which had felt to Rosa like a tacit agreement that dancing with his cousin was not such a great idea. A second later the two boys had disappeared.

'Aren't you going to look?' said Lito, with an impatience in his voice that Rosa found even more surprising. Since she had turned sixteen, no boy had spoken to her with anything less than the utmost courtesy.

'I'm on my way to school,' Rosa replied.

'I know. I see you walk to school most mornings. Sometimes I'm on my boat, too far out at sea. You're just a dot on the beach. But most mornings I'm right here, so I see you.'

'Oh . . .'

'It's okay. I don't expect you to have noticed me. I just thought you'd find this interesting.'

'Find what interesting?'

'Well.' Lito shrugged. 'Either you look or you don't.'

Rosa hesitated, then walked over the sand towards him. As

she approached, he picked up a T-shirt and slung it across his left shoulder so that it hung over one side of his chest. Only then did he turn to face her.

'So,' said Rosa.

Lito pointed at the water in the plastic container. 'You have to see from up close. You have to get closer.'

Rosa squatted.

'There. Now follow my finger. You see this very small fry?'

' . . . Yes.'

'You see anything strange about it?'

'No.'

'What do you see?'

' . . . Actually, I can see two fry.'

'No, you *think* you can see two fry, swimming next to each other. But it isn't two. It's one fry, and he has two tails . . .' Lito frowned. 'I've been catching these fry since *I* was a fry, and I've never seen anything like it. I thought maybe something happened to his mother. She might have been hit or bitten by a larger fish when she was pregnant. Some kind of shock . . .'

'Since you were a fry?' said Rosa, and laughed. Then she frowned, puzzled rather than annoyed. 'Is that what was interesting?'

'Yes.' Lito's expression became suddenly alarmed, and he tugged at a fold on his draped T-shirt. 'You don't think it's interesting,' he said.

'It's . . . *quite* interesting.'

He didn't seem convinced.

' . . . I'd better get to school.'

'Yes.'

They both stood up, and before Rosa could say anything else, Lito had lifted his net and was walking towards the shallows.

Rosa watched him for a few moments. He wasn't short, but he certainly wasn't tall either, and he was as black as the other boys who worked in the sea. But he was also more handsome and less scarred than many of them, and he cut his hair much shorter. Disco hair was prized by all whose parents permitted it, following the local tradition of diligently matching Manila fashions of the previous year.

Maybe Lito had strict parents. Anyway, avoiding disco hair was no bad thing. Disco hair, Rosa commented to herself as she set off again towards Infanta, looked pretty ridiculous. She hadn't really noticed before, but it wasn't manly at all.

3

At lunch-break, when Leesha had suggested they leave the school grounds to talk in the burnt-out Second World War army truck, Rosa had known that something important had happened. So had Ella, who'd spotted them as they left the playground, and caught up before they vanished into the privacy of the jungle.

Arranging themselves in the cabin, laying palm leaves beneath them to protect their dresses from the rusty seats, there was a sense of anticipation. A few minutes later, it was difficult to imagine how the sense of anticipation could have been better rewarded.

'What?' Ella gasped. 'You did *what*?' She fluttered a hand weakly in front of her face, and nearly knocked her glasses off her nose. 'Quick, I'm dizzy. I may faint.'

'It's the truth,' said Leesha, glowing with happy defiance.

'You realize,' Ella began, but she had to break off to fan herself more vigorously. A series of deep breaths gave her the strength to compose herself. Then, after a pointless glance into the thick foliage that surrounded the truck, she whispered, 'You realize that there's absolutely no going back from this point.'

'Of course. But I don't want to go back. I want to marry him, and he wants to marry me.'

'So he says!'

'I told him. I told him I wasn't an inland girl.'

'And?'

'He told me he wasn't even interested in inland girls.'

'Oh?' said Ella, arching her eyebrows. 'For someone not interested, he's made enough trips over the boondocks.'

'Only to keep Doublon and Simeon company.'

'Mmm-hmm.'

'Mmm-hmm nothing, Ella.'

'Mmm-*hmm*.'

'Mmm-*hmm* nothing! If I didn't trust him, I wouldn't be marrying him.'

'Marriage!' Ella echoed, abruptly changing her tone. 'It's too wonderful for words.'

'I'm telling my parents this evening.'

'This evening! What do you think they'll say?'

'I hope they'll agree to it.'

'But of course they will! Turing is so . . . well! His father virtually *runs* the sawmill.'

'Everyone says he'll be the general manager when Tata Rudy retires.'

Ella widened her eyes. 'And one can only expect that Turing will run the sawmill after his father.'

'Yes,' sighed Leesha. 'But I'm not interested in that. If I could only tell you, Ella, when you're in love, things like sawmills seem so unimportant.'

'It's *too* wonderful!'

A silence began to grow. Rosa waited until it had grown to a suitable length before she cleared her throat and asked, 'What exactly is a blow-job?'

*

The nature of the act was both predictable (Rosa had heard rumours along similar lines) and unexpected (she hadn't thought the rumours were true). Straightforwardly unexpected, however, was that half-way through Leesha's graphic explanation, Lito popped into Rosa's mind. Dismayed, forcing him out again, Rosa told herself it was because she happened to have seen him that morning. He had been registered as something beyond a familiar local face, so his arrival in her mind was without any great meaning. Inevitably she had fleshed out the image, and he was the first boy at hand.

It was an argument that carried no weight, and after the briefest of absences, Lito popped back again. This time, Rosa's dismay was at the rush of jealousy she felt towards Leesha. Then it was at the odd elation that followed, and finally at her own hot cheeks.

Leesha noticed the blush immediately. She read it as innocence. Rosa, twirling the small silver-plated crucifix that hung around her neck, was content to let the mistake go uncorrected.

Chismis, gossip like a soft wind that raises heads from field-work, strong enough to chill sweat. *Chismis* ladies, the ones who excelled in the gossip's collection and distribution. Nobody trusted them, but everybody gave them their confidences and secrets, because taking these things was their art. Ella's art. Since she had been as young as five or six, people had identified Ella as a *chismis* lady in waiting. They said she made up for Coke-bottle glasses and thin lips by having second sight and a big mouth.

When the end-of-school bell rang that afternoon, Leesha's news had already spread beyond the boundaries of Infanta, and was making its way cross-country to her barrio and her house. Rosa followed lazily behind, day-dreaming, keeping half an eye out for any pretty flowers growing by the side of the road.

4

Rosa's father, Doming, wasn't talking over dinner that evening. Nothing unusual – a whole week could go by without him uttering a word. Ever since the dynamite-fishing accident that had deafened him, his communication had become more and more limited, these days restricted mainly to nods, smiles, shrugs and similar gestures. Not that the underwater pulse had damaged anything beyond his hearing – Doming had never been a big talker. Rosa sometimes felt he was closer to his natural self after the accident, rather than before.

Corazon not talking, however, *was* unusual. Normally, Corazon was chatty to the same degree her husband was not, but she hadn't opened her mouth since the three of them had sat down.

Eventually, Rosa became troubled. The quiet was not angry or resentful, but it was certainly loaded, so she decided to find out what it was loaded with. 'Is there something the matter, Mother?' she asked, ladling a cube of chicken neck on to her plate.

Corazon flicked her eyebrows. 'Should something be the matter?'

'I don't know.'

'You don't know?'

'No,' said Rosa, genuinely. 'I don't. Tell me.'

Corazon's eyebrows flicked again. Then she pursed her lips. 'How is your school-work?'

' . . . School-work?'

'Yes, your school-work. How is it?'

'It's fine.'

'Really,' said Corazon. 'Interesting . . . I'd have expected it to be one of the first things to suffer . . .'

Rosa looked over at her father, to see if he was registering any part of this mysterious conversation, but he wasn't. 'Suffer from what?'

'I notice you have a flower in your hair,' Corazon replied, apparently ignoring the question.

Rosa paused. 'I saw it growing near the . . .'

'Naturally. Do I know him?'

' . . . Know him?'

'Do I know the boy? Or am I going to be surprised like Leesha's mother this evening?' Corazon leaned forwards across the table, and the curl to her mouth became an open smile. 'Am I going to be cleaning rice tomorrow afternoon, and feel a little gossip breeze in my ear, telling me that my daughter has become intimate with her future husband!'

Rosa pulled the flower from her hair with one hand, and covered her mouth with the other.

'Is it Mario?'

'No!'

'Gregorio?'

'There's no boy!'

'Fine, fine. Suddenly you're wearing a flower, but there's no boy.' Corazon burst out laughing. 'Let me tell you something. As soon as the first one marries, the others will all follow. Within a few months you'll all be lined up in your best dresses to talk to the padre. It's always been that way. Of course . . .' she sniffed delicately ' . . . I was the first in my *barkada*.'

'There's no boy.'

'I'll be waiting for the little breeze . . .'

'I think you'll be waiting a long time.'

'I think it's Mario.'

'If you're finished eating I'll take the plates outside.'

'Soon it will be someone else's plates!'

*

Lying awake, Rosa became aware of her bed. She'd been sleeping on the same wooden boards for the last six years, and boards of similar dimensions for the years before that – but now she was aware of them. They felt small and hard, and they creaked whenever she shifted her position. Plates, Rosa thought, watching a lizard flicker across the ceiling. Plates, bed . . . One wouldn't change without the other.

'Angel!' Doming had shouted earlier, as Rosa had slipped behind the curtain partition that separated her room from the rest of the house. Rosa had stuck her head back around the curtain, wondering what had made him break his customary silence.

'What?' she mouthed.

'Why did you take that flower out of your hair!' he yelled, making Corazon cup her hands over her ears. 'It looked very pretty! You put in another one tomorrow!'

'Maybe.'

'Did you say something, angel?'

Rosa held up the oil-lamp to her face so Doming could see her lips. 'Maybe,' she repeated. 'If I see a nice one on the way to school.'

'Keep a look out on the way to school! You might see a nice one!'

'Okay.'

'Good-night then, angel!'

'Yes. Good-night.'

5

At a certain point, for a limited time, dead things turn black and pink. People and animals, black where the skin is exposed, and where the black skin flakes or splits, bright pink shines beneath. This is when dead things smell the worst. The stench has an impact, and constricts the throat muscles to stop the lungs from taking in any more bad air, while also preventing the lungs from letting the bad air out.

Trapped inside Rosa, a sense of death spread from her chest at the speed an oil droplet spreads on water. In a second, it had infected her whole body. She took quick steps, and held off taking a breath until she was sure that the breath would be fresh. But she misjudged the zone of the stench, and her quick steps only brought her closer to the source. A pig, bloated by the sea, a quarter submerged in the sand, left by the three a.m. tide.

'It must have washed up during the night,' said Lito. 'I saw you walking down the beach. I should have warned you.' One of his hands hovered an inch above her back, ready to reassure Rosa if she was sick again, too shy for the meantime to go the extra mile. The other held the flower she'd picked and dropped as she stumbled away from the shore, aiming blindly for the tree-line. 'Look, the flower's okay. You can put it back.'

Rosa gazed at the patch of ground and splashes of breakfast between her hands. 'Keep it,' she said, too disorientated and humiliated to think about what she was saying. 'It was for you anyway.'

'The flower was for me?'

'I wore it for you.'

'. . . Why?'

'I don't know,' said Rosa, and spat.

Lito hesitated, not sure what to say.

'I need to wipe my mouth.' Rosa looked up. Lito was wearing his T-shirt draped over his left shoulder like a towel – the same way he'd worn it yesterday when she'd walked over to inspect his mutant milkfish. 'Can I use your shirt? I have to wipe my mouth. I can't go to school like this.'

Lito frowned. 'Um,' he said, still hesitating.

'Is it clean?'

'Yes.'

'I'll rinse it in the sea afterwards.'

'No, I'll rinse it.'

'So . . .?'

He handed it to her, and at the same time moved a pace to the side so that her back was to him. He was either putting himself out of view, or politely letting Rosa dab away the vomit in relative privacy.

She murmured her thanks.

The T-shirt smelled strongly of soap. He must have washed it the night before, which seemed curious, given that this was the shirt he worked in. And the T-shirt was old, frayed on the collar stitching, but was as bright and white as it would have been when new.

Rosa finished wiping, then flipped the T-shirt over to take one last deep breath within the clean folds, ridding herself of the pig's final traces. Then she held it up for Lito to take, and when she'd stood and turned to face him, it was back over his shoulder.

Rosa thought for a moment. 'Actually, I want to rinse it for you.'

'I can do it. Won't you be late for school?'

'No.'

'Well, anyway . . .'

'Well, anyway, I'm going to rinse it,' said Rosa, making up her mind. 'It's the least I can do.'

He flinched as she reached out. She had known he would.

Lito's right pectoral muscle existed, and his left one did not. It was absent. With only a thin covering of skin, his ribcage was

94

visible all the way up his chest, until it dipped beneath his collar-bone. The absence of the muscle was compounded by an overdeveloped right pectoral and left shoulder. Bluntly concave where it should have been convex, Lito's torso was deformed.

'It's a good job you did all your throwing up already,' said Lito, with a hopelessly nervous laugh.

Rosa waited before replying. 'You look like a bar of chocolate,' she said eventually. 'A bar someone took a bite out of. Your ribs are the teeth marks.'

His eyes flicked downwards, then at the T-shirt, then downwards again.

'You're embarrassed.'

He nodded.

'You shouldn't be.' Rosa lifted her hand and gave him a soft nudge on the arm. 'It isn't so bad to be a bar of chocolate.'

Sandmen

I

It isn't so bad. Rosa had said the same thing to Raphael, when he was old enough for them to explain what had happened to him, and why. It isn't so bad to be a bar of chocolate.

What she should have added, if she was being truthful, was that it might not be bad but it was hard. Being deformed would make his life harder than it would otherwise have been. And then she should have added that bad, and even good, were irrelevant anyway. Hard was what really mattered.

'*ER!*'

'Yes,' Rosa called back, although it was difficult to think of anything she wanted to do less than watch *ER*, other than watch it with her mother. 'I'm coming.'

'You missed the beginning section! Already I'm confused about what's going on!'

'At the beginning they only show what happened the week before. The announcer says, "*Previously on* ER". Something like that.'

'No.' Corazon waved a finger. '"*Previously on* ER" comes first,' she said, also using the English. 'But then they have an introduction to the new story. Look, the credits have passed now. So you have missed "*Previously*", and also the introduction.'

'I'm sure we'll be able to pick it up.'

Drugs and dosages, procedures, relationships between doctors and nurses, short-tempered surgeons – Rosa was impressed every time she watched the hospital programme. The writers did their research. The only thing it lacked was a certain kind of detail. Background people. Not much interested in the plot lines, Rosa studied the background people, looking for familiar expressions and postures, and always found them missing. Not the injured – the ghost faces. The almost translucent figures, drifting, hovering, slumped in chairs. Unfocused eyes, lips pulled back in a strangely vague rictus of horror. She couldn't believe an Accident & Emergency ward existed without them.

And there weren't many gunshot wounds, but maybe Chicago didn't have a problem with gangsters.

'Is the little Negro boy going to die?' asked Corazon, ten minutes in.

Rosa made a quick diagnosis, partly based on medical knowledge and partly based on the boy's role within this week's story. Broken rib, possible punctured lung, angelic face, abusive father, addict mother on a rehab programme. The boy was being cared for by the *guapo* doctor. Or rather, the most *guapo* doctor. 'He shouldn't. Not unless there's some kind of complication.'

'You never know with *ER*! Often there's a complication! Even in rich American hospitals, with all the latest facilities, the children often die! There's no guarantees with *ER*.' Corazon shivered. 'I remember once there was another child, a girl, and she had AIDS. Imagine that.'

Rosa was spared her imagination, to the extent that imagination was required, by the phone ringing. 'I'll get it,' she said, jumping up. 'I'll take it in the kitchen.'

'Let it ring! How can you drag yourself away?'

'It might be work. Maybe an . . . emergency.'

'Nonsense. You know who it is as well as I do.'

'I'll check anyway.'

'If you insist. Actually, you're lucky. I think there's a commercial break coming up soon, but it won't last long.'

'Commercial break,' said Rosa, over her shoulder, already out the door. 'Right.'

2

'Hi,' said her husband. 'I only called to say I'm in the car. Coming home.'

'Are you over United Nations Avenue yet?'

'Just about to reach it.'

'Well . . . don't hang up yet.'

Rosa pictured him. He would have one arm out the driver's window, keeping away the street beggars and vendors with a wave of his cigarette. His other hand would be holding his mobile phone. In the early evening traffic, there would be no need for him to keep a grip on the wheel. He would be creeping the car forward with little pushes of the accelerator.

'Do you have either of your hands on the wheel?'

'Nope . . . Why do you ask?'

'Wondered. That's all.'

'Okay.'

For a short while, the two of them listened to the other one's noise. A ripple of car horns and revved engines for Rosa, and sighs for her husband – just audible above the mobile's fuzz.

'You all right, Rose?' he said after the third sigh, and added, 'Corazon's driving you crazy,' before she could answer.

'It's the same old stuff, but I don't know, for some reason she's really getting to me tonight. We had an argument. She brought up Sarap, and it got me thinking . . .'

'You've got to ignore her, Rose.'

'I can't. Especially not at the kids' bedtime.'

'Raffy can handle it, petal.'

'He shouldn't have to handle things at that age.'

'He'll be fine, stem.'

'Stem.' Rosa smiled. 'How about thorn?'

'I don't like thorns, root.'

' . . . I think I'd rather be a thorn than a root.'

'Well, I think your mother got all the thor–' He broke off. 'Uh-oh,' he muttered. Then there was a pause. ' . . . Oh, no. Oh, *fuck*! I don't *believe* it!'

'What?' said Rosa anxiously.

'Two kids! Two fucking street kids! They put . . . *You little bastards! Sons of fucking whores! Get back here you little . . .*'

'What's happened?'

'Jesus.' There was a click of a car door. 'Yep . . . Yep! They did it all right!'

'Did *what*?'

'I've got a flat. They put nails under the wheel.' He was interrupted by a sudden series of car-horn blasts. *'I've got a flat, you half-breeds! What am I holding you up from? Two whole metres of clear road!'* The car horns continued. *'As soon as I pull over you'll really be able to open up! Pedal to the floor!'*

'Honey, calm. Get the car off the road.'

'Those people!'

'I know. Please, just get the car off the road and change the tyre.'

'Jesus! I just wanted to get home! I'm ten minutes' fucking drive away, and now I'm going to be so *late*!'

'I know.'

'I'm going to have to hang up. Jesus! Those fucking street kids!'

'They're gone. All you can do is change the tyre.'

' . . . Yes.'
'Okay.'
'Okay.'
He hung up.

Rosa looked down the hall and watched the blue TV light,
glowing through the living-room doorway. Then she turned
back into the kitchen, flicked on the kettle, and opened the freezer.
Half-litre tub of Magnolia, halo-halo.

3

After calling for the third time, Corazon appeared to resign
herself to watching *ER* alone. Rosa felt bad – it could surprise
her that whatever else she felt towards her mother, the strongest
feeling was love – but not bad enough to move from the kitchen.
There would be time to make it up to her later.

So she drank her coffee, scooped at the halo-halo ice-cream,
and ran her eyes over the crossword she had left unfinished
during her lunch-break.

'Do you always sit here, *po*?'
Rosa had a quick look around the sea front and the park. It
was a category of reflex action – she knew where she was, and
knew that she always sat on the same bench, but she was checking
anyway. For the benefit of the small old man who had asked the
question.

'Yes, *po*,' she said, once she had established that the moored
cargo ships, threadbare palm trees and bleached grass were just
as they always were.

The old man scratched his balding head. 'Me too, *po*. Usually from around eleven to eleven thirty. But I'm late today, so I've missed my spot.'

'There's plenty of room. I can move all this.' She slid her newspaper and lunch over to the side.

'That's very civil of you, *po.*'

'Not at all, *po.* I shouldn't take up so much space with my sandwiches. Perhaps you'd like one?'

'Thank you,' he said. 'But my teeth aren't up to sandwiches. I have a sweet rice cake to eat.' And he produced a parcel from somewhere inside his shirt. 'Don't let me interrupt you from your crossword.'

'Oh, I was getting stuck with it anyway.'

'Give me a clue.'

'Um, okay . . .' Rosa glanced at the blank boxes. 'Cried over spilt milk. Six letters, third letter is a . . .'

'*Sayang,*' said the old man cheerfully.

'*Sayang*. It fits, *po* . . .'

'*Sayang*. That's what I say whenever I spill some milk.' He cackled. 'With these weak wrists and fingers, I say "*sayang*" several times a day! Give me another.'

'Okay . . . Number of the knife, two words, six and five . . .'

'*Byenté nwébe.*'

Rosa filled it in, shaking her head. 'Of course. It's so obvious. I see ten *byenté nwébe* cuts a day, for goodness' sake. And *byenté* fits with *sayang.*'

'There, *doctora,*' said the old man, and beamed. 'Now I won't do any more. I don't want to ruin your crossword.'

'You aren't ruining it at all, *po!*'

'You're very kind. Anyway, you're impressed with me at the moment. But if I don't get the next clue, you'll be less impressed. So I'd prefer to leave it at that.' He winked at her. 'You can see, I'm very sly.'

'Yes, *po,*' said Rosa, laughing. 'So you are.'

The old man took a slow munch of his rice cake. Then, after a somewhat laborious swallow, he said, 'You're a pure Tagalog. Quezon province.'

Rosa nodded. 'You are too, *po*.'

'You know Infanta?'

'I grew up near Infanta, *po*.'

'I grew up on Polillo.'

'On a clear day, I could see Polillo from my house.'

'Yes . . . That's why we come to this park to eat lunch. A little bit of sea, a few coconut trees.' He held up his bony hands to the side of his face. 'If you put your hands like this, and gaze in certain directions, you will only be able to see trees and sea, and you can pretend you are home.'

'Apart from the smell and the sounds, *po*.'

'Heh. The smells and the sounds . . . and the sea is as filthy as the piss channel from a pigsty, and the trees have grey leaves.' The old man took an even slower mouthful from his rice cake, and chewed it – mournfully, Rosa thought. Then he kicked his slipper off his right foot, and made a trace in the dust and cigarette butts with his toes. 'I hate this city. I've been here thirty years, and I never liked it for even one minute. Where I live, there is no green except in the plants that grow between the concrete cracks. Is it like that where you live?'

'No, *po*. In many ways, my area is quite pretty. There are plenty of trees and flowers, and at the moment, lots of blossom.'

'Ah, blossom. That's nice. But . . . it's not like home.'

'No, *po*,' said Rosa firmly. 'It is certainly not like home.'

'You regret leaving.'

'No. Or, I don't know. I mean . . .' Rosa's eyebrows knotted in concentration. 'I have much more in Manila than I ever dreamed I would have. I'm a doctor, my children go to a good school, I have a big house. A car . . . These things are not what I expected from life.'

'I think you do miss home.'

' . . . Yes, *po*.'

'You came here to study?'

'Yes.'

'To study,' said the old man, and he tilted his head. 'But that's not all.'

' . . . No.'

'There was another reason. And it's not a happy story.'

Rosa didn't reply. With amazing speed, tears had appeared in her eyes and were now rolling down her cheeks. 'Oh,' she said, and reached down to get a packet of tissues from her bag. 'This is so . . . I don't know why I suddenly . . .' When she found the tissues, she sat up again, but the packet remained unopened on her lap. 'Sorry, *po*.'

'Ah.' Squinting at her against the sunshine, he took her hand and gave it a soft squeeze. 'There . . . There it is. Thirty years I've been here. Nobody comes to this city with a happy story.'

'*Sayang.*'

Rosa traced over her earlier ink marks, thickening the letters. The coffee was cold, the ice-cream was melting, and something warm had nestled against her leg. It had been there for a couple of minutes.

' . . . Out of interest, why aren't you in bed, Raffy?'

Two eyes appeared over the top of the table. 'I'm not tired at all.'

'Come here, then. Let's have a look at you.' Holding him under the arms, she lifted him on to her knee. He wriggled slightly, getting into the most comfortable position. 'Are you after ice-cream?'

'No. Where's Dad?'

'Stuck near United Nations Avenue. You want to call him?'

'Yes.'

'Pass me the phone and I'll dial the number.'

Three rings. 'I'm going to be a while yet, Rose,' said a gruff voice. 'I can't get the wheel nuts off. It's like they've been welded on.'

'I've got someone who wants to speak to you.'

'Someone who's still wide awake, way past their bedtime?'

'Could be . . .'

'Male? Female?'

'Guess.'

'All right.' There was the clank of a tyre-spanner repeatedly hitting a kerbstone. Then a calm voice. 'Put him on.'

4

'Hello, big guy. I hear you can't sleep.'

'Hi, Dad. Can't sleep.'

'That's what I hear.'

'It's pretty hot tonight, and a mosquito got through my netting even though Mum covered the hole. More than one mosquito, actually.'

'I never understood how mosquitoes always find the hole.'

'They *always* do!'

'It never fails. But you can sleep with a few mosquitoes, Raffy. Remember when we visit relatives in the provinces? If you can deal with those country mosquitoes, these little city ones shouldn't be any trouble.'

'Hmm. What's up with you, anyway? Why aren't you home yet?'

'Late getting away from work. Got a tribunal coming up for some Jap clients. And I got a flat. Changing it right now.'

'You got a flat tyre on the car?'

'Uh-huh.'

'Do you need any help changing it? I could come and . . .'

'I think I'd rather have you tucked up in bed. But thanks for the offer. Now, tell me, did you say a prayer before turning in?'

'Uh . . . no.'

'Did you forget?'

'Mmm.'

'Right. So maybe that's why you couldn't drift off. Maybe you should say it now.'

'I couldn't drift off because I didn't say the prayer?'

'Sounds like it.'

'God was stopping me?'

' . . . Sure.'

'Really?'

'Yes. So if you say it now, you'll be able to get some rest.'

'Why didn't he stop my chest being burned?'

' . . . It wasn't God who burned your chest.'

'He couldn't stop my chest being burned?'

'He could, but . . .'

'He cares more about sleep?'

'Okay, Raffy. I'm changing a tyre over here. How about you say the prayer?'

Raphael paused, then cleared his throat.

> 'As I lay me down to sleep,
> I pray the Lord my soul to keep.
> If I should die before I wake,
> I pray the Lord my soul to take.'

'That's good, Raffy.'

'I don't feel tired yet.'

'Give it a few minutes. Go on, you go up to bed. I'll come and say hello when I get back, and if you still aren't asleep, maybe we can talk a little.'

'What if God's got me sleeping by then?'
'I'll let him get on with it.'
' . . . Okay.'
'Good-night, then.'
'Yes. Good-night.'

5

The pak-pak of gunfire jolted Rosa's body and made her hands tighten around Raphael's shoulders. It was a volley of four or five shots, and in the brief lull that followed, Corazon appeared at the bottom of the stairs.

'Where from?'

Rosa looked around. ' . . . Let me get Raphael in bed.'

'Shooting!' said Raphael. '*Wow!* Do you think it's close?'

'It's miles away. And it's not going to stop you from going to . . .'

The second volley was longer and more intense. From the rippled rhythm, there were at least two guns, small-arms fire.

'I think it's from the direction of the squatter camps,' said Corazon quickly.

'The squatter camps?' Raphael was breathless with excitement. 'That's not miles away at all, Mum! That's just down the road!'

Lita emerged from her door, blinking at the light. 'Mum? There's shooting . . .'

The third volley made Rosa think of a dry kindling stack, abruptly engulfed in flame.

Lita started crying. Raphael's gleeful expression became immediately doubtful, and then he started crying too.

'Angels, angels,' said Corazon, coming up the stairs. 'What's to be afraid of? Rosa is perfectly right. The shooting sounds much closer than it really is.'

Both kids looked at their mother, but Rosa was too alarmed now to be able to disguise it.

'Come on, little ones.' Corazon bustled past, and started ushering the children back to their bedroom. 'I'll sing to you if you hurry up.'

'Thanks, Mother,' said Rosa to the empty landing, moments later. She was still standing in the same spot, when two final gunshots sounded. Different from the others. Not as contained, less muffled, more isolated, and somehow more deliberate. A person had been killed with those shots.

'So let that be the end of it,' she whispered. And for the next few minutes, the only noise to be heard was Corazon's song about dreaming dreams and the Sandman.

Locked and Lost

I

Rosa and Lito lay on a cheap blanket bought in the Infanta open market, her head on his stomach and his hand stroking her hair. School-books, fine netting, plastic container and clothes were placed neatly to the side. The leaves and branches around them were like four walls and a roof. The surf kept an easy rhythm.

'Are you comfortable?' said Lito quietly.

Rosa nodded. 'What about my head here? It's not too heavy?'

'It's fine.'

'I can move.'

'It's the nicest thing I can think of, your head there.'

'Good . . .' Rosa turned her face enough to kiss him lightly on the solar plexus. 'Rubbing alcohol,' she whispered, and kissed him again. 'Smells sweet.'

'Like chocolate?'

' . . . Just something sweet.'

Split coconut shells and husks gave a light perfume to the forest floor. Sand, blown through the tree-line, gave the topsoil a dusty warmth. Strips of morning sunlight, cutting through the foliage, left gold tiger-markings where they hit brown skin.

2

School-work, one of the first things to suffer. Not surprising, considering how much time Rosa spent gazing out of the classroom's glassless windows. Glassless windows led to the orange dirt of the school-yard, which led to a short stretch of road and a couple of outlying Infanta houses, which led to shadows shifting in the jungle and the cloud formations above them. A world of day-dreams was never closer.

'Are you concentrating, Rosa?'

Yes, concentrating hard. But on a memory of clutching Lito tight in her arms and legs, as opposed to mathematics. In this more interesting equation, one plus one could resolve itself as three.

'Perhaps you could tell the class the name of the man who founded the Liga Filipina?'

Lito if it was a boy, Lita if it was a girl. Rosa had decided on the names after the first time they had slept with each other.

'Where does the American president live?'

In a nipa hut, not much different to the one in which she was raised. Unlike Leesha, Rosa had no great ambitions for herself or her future husband. A nipa hut and a small garden would do fine.

'Describe the function of the heart.'

Rosa blinked, turned from the window, and gave her teacher a quizzical frown. She didn't know where to begin.

Rosa and Leesha sat on the low wall that separated the edge of the playground from the dirt-track road. To their left a few boys bounced a basketball. Each time one of the older boys shot a hoop or made a steal, they would glance over at the two girls to see if they had been noticed, and remained cheerfully undiscouraged when they saw that they had not. To Rosa and Leesha's right, a small group of eight- to twelve-year-olds swung a skipping-rope. The chant was Black Dog.

'In our day,' said Leesha, 'Tata Ilad was Black Dog. That poor little old man, looking after his pineapple rows, and we always said he was Black Dog.'

'I almost never made it to Tata Ilad. I'd have tripped by the sixth or seventh verse.'

'Seventh verse . . . Was that the dead chickens? "Seven dead chickens, laid on the ground, grandmother counts them, one-two-three . . ." Wasn't that it?'

'No,' said Rosa, after a hesitation to remember the lines. 'It was six chickens. Seventh verse was Black Dog looking in the windows. Remember, he looks in seven windows at the sleeping kids.'

'Yes!' said Leesha. 'Oh, I could *never* trip on that verse! I always used to say to myself, if I trip, then when I have children, one of them will be chosen as the seventh kid!'

'Naturally. I said the same thing to myself, but it didn't work because I'd get too nervous. I remember going home one day, crying to my mother that Black Dog would be coming for my children.'

'What did she say?'

'She took me straight to the padre, and he blessed me. Then she made him do it again, to make sure. Then she made me promise never to skip that chant again.'

'Mmm. Quite a strong reaction.'

'She said that when she was a girl, she met two Visayans who had seen Black Dog with their own eyes. And they were new to Luzon, so they didn't know the story already.'

'But you must have skipped it again after that. We were always skipping that chant.'

'Yes, I did.' Rosa laughed a little shyly. 'Actually, I'd deliberately trip on the chickens. Who cares about a few chickens?'

Leesha nodded. 'True.'

'We didn't have any chickens, anyway . . .'

At that moment, the ball from the boys' game rolled towards where the two girls sat and came to rest against Leesha's leg. With one apologetic arm raised, the oldest boy, Sison, trotted over.

'Sorry,' he said.

Leesha kicked the ball away, planning to send it towards the rope-skippers, but it hit the side of her foot and ended up spinning back towards him. She gave a little snort of annoyance.

'I suppose you think we've been impressed with the way you've been playing. You think we've been watching you out of the corners of our eyes, and that's why we're sitting here on this wall. To watch you.'

Sison scratched his head.

'But, you know, we aren't at all interested in seeing you show off.'

'Well,' he said, as he picked up the ball and began walking back to his friends. 'We know you aren't, Leesha, because you'll be married soon.' Then, somewhat bravely, he glanced back at Rosa. 'But not everyone will be married soon.'

'. . . To be fair, he has a point,' Leesha whispered when Sison broke into a jog. The ball bounced loyally by his side, snapping upwards as if the earth's gravity had temporarily relocated itself to the palm of his hand. 'You don't have a boyfriend, and . . .' She gave a business-like sigh. ' . . . Sison *is* fantastically handsome.'

Rosa looked surprised. 'Leesha, you can't say things like that! What about Turing?'

'I'm only stating what's obvious. He's gorgeous.'

'Lee*sha*!'

'It's for your sake I'm pointing this out, Rosie. I couldn't care less about his dreamy lips. I mean, don't you find him attractive?'

'No.'

'Why not?'

'Disco hair,' said Rosa briefly. Then added, 'Although I think disco hair looks *very* good on Turing.'

Leesha chuckled. 'I don't. Turing doesn't know it yet, but the first thing I'm going to do after our wedding day is get out my scissors and cut it off.'

They both looked at each other.

'And I might give him a haircut too,' Leesha added a beat later, and Rosa collapsed into giggles.

Orange school-yard dirt collected on the basketball players' feet and calves. A trio of men and their machetes appeared on the jungle fringe, then disappeared back inside. Clouds found new formations and rolled across the sky at deceptive speed.

'Anyway,' said Rosa, a little louder and less casually than she had intended. When she tried again, she had dropped her voice. 'Anyway, perhaps I don't find Sison attractive because I have a boyfriend already.'

'Ssst!' said Leesha immediately, and put a finger to her lips. Then she scanned the playground, lifted up both feet and checked beneath them, and made a cursory inspection of the long grass on the road-side of the wall. Finally, she lifted the collar of her T-shirt and peeked inside. 'Okay, Ella is nowhere to be seen. Who is he?'

'I only said per*haps*.'

'Oh, I know exactly what you said.'

'No, really.'

'No, really, I know exactly what you said.'

This time, Rosa's giggles were pure nerves and ended as abruptly as they had begun. She took a deep breath, realizing as she did so that this was the first time she had ever spoken his name outside of his company.

'Lito . . .' Leesha echoed, furrowing her brow as she tried to put a face to the name. 'Lito, Lito . . . He doesn't go to school?'

'No.'

'He's not the boy from the Infanta chemist? The Ilocano?'

'No, no. The Lito from the next barrio. He has his own boat. In the morning, he's always fishing on the beach near the Abiawin church.'

' . . . *That* Lito?'

'Yes. His boat is the one with the painted . . .'

'I know who you're talking about,' Leesha interrupted, her expression becoming unambiguously serious. 'Tata Vin's son.'

'Did you know Tata Vin?'

'I think my father knew him, but . . .' The sentence was cut short as Leesha raised a hand to her cheek. 'You and Lito . . . You've, what, fallen in love already?'

'Leesha, I now understand *everything* about how you feel for Turing.'

'You've slept with him.'

'We'll get married.'

'Your parents don't know.'

'I love him completely!'

' . . . Completely.'

'Aren't . . . aren't you pleased for me? You don't seem . . . very pleased for me.'

'Rosie,' said Leesha absently, more to herself. Then she appeared to refocus. 'Of course I'm pleased for you. I was surprised, that's all. I had no idea you'd found someone, and . . .'

' . . . And?'

But the focus slipped again. ' . . . And I think you're so *pretty*. You're one of the . . . No, you're *the* prettiest girl in the whole Infanta area. My God, probably the whole of Luzon. All of these boys, they would swim to Polillo for you. Sison would climb the Sierra Madre on his hands and . . .'

'Sison?'

' . . . knees.'

'Leesha, what are you saying? I don't understand at *all*.'

'I . . . I'm not saying anything. I'm being stupid.' She shook her head. 'Rosie.'

'Yes?'

'I'm being *stupid*.' Leesha smiled. ' . . . Falling in love. It is amazing, isn't it?'

'Yes it is!' said Rosa, wondering why the smile made sweat prick between her shoulder-blades.

'It's amazing, and I'm so pleased for you, of course.'

3

The sudden downpour that evening was as unexpected as a fist-fight in a church, and was strong enough to tear branches from palm trees. But even the power of the rain, and the crack and brightness of the lightning, seemed a desultory warning of the winds that followed. By nightfall, it had become the kind of typhoon that could lift a house and spin it across a paddy-field.

Sitting in a pool of oil-lamp light, held securely in Corazon's arms, Rosa could feel her mother's lips moving against her ear, but over the sound of the storm she couldn't hear the words. '*Dios mío*,' Rosa imagined. Corazon would be using a Spanish prayer, because where God was concerned, she believed Spanish was the language most likely to produce results. '*Por favor, dé su protección a esta casita y esta familia*.'

A fresh peal of thunder, which sounded as if the entire structure of the sky was breaking away from its horizon seam, made

Corazon's hold tighten. Rosa dared to open her eyes for a moment, and saw a strobe of white slashes against the dark walls of her home. The typhoon was peering through the gaps in the nipa matting. Nestled further into her mother's embrace, Rosa decided not to open her eyes again until the slashes were caused by daylight.

But daylight never really came. Hours later, the only indication of sun-up was Doming waking. He had slept better than his wife and daughter, untroubled by the shattering noise. As he stretched his muscles, Corazon gently extricated herself from her daughter's curled form, and walked over to the kitchen area to fix some breakfast.

Rosa watched her father gauge the storm by leaning against the front door and feeling it vibrate through his shoulders. A flick of his eyebrows conceded that they were locked in for the day. After a few minutes of drumming his fingers on his belly, he was seated at their small wobbly table, frowning at his stubby fingers. Fish-hooks were lined up to his left, strips of blue thread were lined up to his right, and threaded fishhooks were rapidly lining up in front of him.

Rosa helped Doming until mid-morning. Then she helped him sharpen some of his knives. Then some of Corazon's. In the afternoon, Doming fixed the wobbly table and the family spent the rest of the day playing *pusoy dos*, even though the pack was short the two of diamonds.

The next twenty-four hours were much the same, the one variety being the nature of the chores. And so were the next. The only difference to the fourth day was Rosa's realization that if she didn't see Lito soon, she was going to go crazy.

4

'It's out of the question. You'll be brained by a coconut.'

'There won't be any coconuts left on the trees, and the winds have died down.'

'Died down?' Corazon cupped a hand to her ear. 'Died *down*? You're as deaf as your father. Are you telling me you can't hear that . . . that *jet aeroplane* outside our front door?'

'What I can hear is you talking, so the winds must have died down.'

'Don't be smart. It isn't clever to be smart.'

'But . . .'

'No! If Leesha wants her school-books, she must come and get them herself.'

'*I* borrowed them off *her*. I was supposed to give them back the next morning. That was *days* ago.'

'So?'

'So she'll be extremely behind in her work,' said Rosa, using the mystery of modern schooling to throw her mother. 'And she won't be able to pass her exams.'

'She doesn't need "exams" if she's marrying Turing.'

'She's going to be a schoolteacher.'

'She doesn't *need* to be a schoolteacher.'

'Turing *wants* her to be a schoolteacher. It's important to him and . . .'

'I doubt that very much,' Corazon interrupted, but Rosa could hear the doubt creeping into her voice. She was aware of how nervous Corazon would be of causing any difficulty for such a locally celebrated marriage arrangement. 'But if Leesha needs her precious books so badly, your father can take them round.'

'I see,' said Rosa confidently. 'And can you mime "Take these books to Leesha?"'

' . . . Of course I can mime it.'

'Good. How?'

'Well, now. It's perfectly simple. He knows Leesha's name, and where she lives.'

'Ah. But he doesn't know that while Leesha's parents are in Cardona to make wedding preparations, Leesha is staying with her aunt's friend's brother. Who lives in Infanta.'

'Aunt's friend's *brother*? Who on earth is that?'

'Just the brother of a friend of . . .'

' . . . her aunt's.'

Rosa nodded. 'He had enough room to take in all the kids.'

For a couple of moments, Corazon looked at her husband, who was painstakingly drawing two diamonds on a small rectangle of cardboard. 'God,' she muttered. 'Why did I marry someone who can't read?'

In truth, the winds had died down a good deal since the typhoon had been at its strongest – otherwise Corazon would never have let Rosa go. But they were still strong enough to make walking difficult, especially with her wet skirt acting as a sail. Alternately, the material would balloon and jerk her sideways, or empty of air and whip around the sides of her legs.

She ditched the school-books a few hundred metres from her house, hiding them under a flat stone. They were soaked, but the pencil marks would survive. Anyway, Leesha had about as much interest in passing exams as in becoming a schoolteacher – which was to say, no interest at all. Rosa had only taken the books because otherwise they would have been thrown away or used by Leesha's grandfather for cigarette papers, and it would have been a pity to waste the unused pages. Now they had been put to a better use than she could have possibly considered, so it had all worked out very well.

Her single worry was how, once she got to Lito's house, she

would manage to let him know that she was there. Knocking on his front door would mean meeting his family, and ending the clandestine nature of their relationship. She didn't feel ready for that yet. For no reasons beyond instinct, she suspected that Corazon would need some groundwork prepared before any declarations were made. Leesha's reaction had confirmed as much.

In any case, she needn't have worried. As she neared the point of the beach where they always met, she spotted a slim figure through the driving rain, with an immediately recognizable lop-sided stance.

Rosa never found out how Lito had known the exact moment to wait for her. She hoped he might have been waiting since the typhoon had broken, or that they shared a special lovers' tele-pathy. But the opportunity to ask didn't arise, locked and lost in his embrace and kiss.

5

Doming had walked into the house with blood streaming out of his ears and mouth, and bright red eyes. Glass from the bottle that had held the dynamite peppered his chest and forehead. It was a miracle he hadn't also been blinded. The expression on his face said plainly that he had absolutely no idea what had just happened to him. He must have found his way back home on autopilot. The expression, and the autopilot, had remained for months after. The shock had been very great. Dynamite exploding a metre in front of him – a very great shock.

Rosa saw Ella over Lito's shoulder. Almost hidden through the leaves, rain running down the lenses of her Coke-bottle glasses, mouth in a perfect 'oh'. She was squatting with her dress hiked up around her thighs, as if she were going to the toilet. But she couldn't have been. Her house was a ten-minute walk away. She must have seen Rosa pass by, and followed. She must have realized that Rosa's excursion into the tail-end of the typhoon had a motive behind it, the kind worth spying on. *Chismis* ladies understood these things.

Ella fled, even before Rosa managed to cry out and roll Lito off her. Ella and her knowledge, out of reach.

Rosa burst out of the tree-line on to the cold wet sand of the beach. Standing naked in the downpour, she shook her fists at the already distant figure, and shouted, 'Thief!' Then, more desperate than angry, 'Come back!' The figure hesitated for a moment, to look back over its shoulder, then picked up its pace.

Perro Mío

I

Rosa stood in the kitchen with the telephone receiver to her ear. At twenty- to thirty-second intervals, she pressed the disconnect button, then pressed the redial button straight after. The time it took the exchange to establish its link to a mobile was a free fall of hope and frustration. The hard landing was the recorded message that explained her husband's phone was switched off, when Rosa knew perfectly well that it wasn't. Twice there had been a couple of rings before the link had inexplicably failed. Low power at the transmitter station, or low batteries in the mobile, or just bad luck – which was why each hit of the redial button was making her more anxious. Rosa took bad luck as seriously as she took anything. She had seen enough people, inside and outside her professional life, hurt by nothing except things happening in a way they normally didn't.

'This time,' she said, redialling again. 'This time.'

'Rose?' said her husband's voice, and it sounded extraordinarily faint and far away.

'Yes! Thank God I've got through. I've been getting worried.'

' . . . I can hardly hear you, sweetheart.'

'I said I've been getting worried! There's been some shooting in the area tonight, somewhere quite near by. We're all perfectly okay here, but I think you should be careful driving home. In fact, maybe you should even wait a while.'

There was a silence that lasted several seconds. Then her husband said, 'Rose? Are you there? I can hardly hear you.'

'I said . . .'

'Could you speak up?'

Rosa raised her voice. 'I said you have to be *careful* driving home. I think maybe you should *wait* a while. There's been *shooting* near by.'

There was another silence. 'I've nearly got the tyre fixed.'

' . . . What?'

'Those wheel nuts. Jesus.'

'No, *listen*, Sonny! In the streets near by! There's been shooting . . .'

'It won't be long before I can start driving back.'

'I said, *don't* drive back!'

'Hardly hear you, sweetheart. You're just a noise.'

'Hello?'

'Just a fuzz.'

'Sonny! Can you hear me at all?'

'Anyway, if you can hear me, then . . .'

'Sonny, will you *listen*! You've got to *wait* before coming home!'

' . . . I've nearly got the car fixed, and I'll be home pretty soon.'

'*No!*' Rosa shouted. '*Listen to me!*' And her husband's voice was swallowed by the static.

2

'I heard you shouting. You shouldn't have been shouting. I was trying to calm the kids, trying to sing to them and make them calm enough to sleep, and you can't make a little child calm when they can hear their mother shouting.'

Rosa nodded. 'I know. I'm sorry. The line . . . I was trying to speak to Sonny, but the line . . .'

'Sonny? He's fixed the tyre? Is he driving home? Didn't you try to stop him?'

'I don't think he could hear me.'

'You can't call him back?'

'I can't get through. I tried so many times and I only got through once. He couldn't hear me, and I couldn't understand what he was saying . . .'

Corazon noticed Rosa's lower lip tense, and gave her daughter a frown of stern concern. 'Now, there's no point in us getting ourselves upset. Sonny is a sensible man and he'll steer clear of any trouble. Anyway, those gunmen will be long gone by now. All that shooting. They won't want to stick around.'

'Yes, that's true,' Rosa agreed, and quickly said it again to make it sound less hollow. 'That's true. They'll want to get out of the area as quickly as possible.'

'Exactly,' said Corazon. Then she spotted the bowl and spoon that Rosa had been using to eat the Magnolia ice-cream. A single bowl and spoon; that could be cleaned with little more than a brief rinse under the tap. 'So let's not sit around and fret. Why don't we do something useful and clean up.'

As Corazon passed Rosa, she brushed a hand against her daughter's arm. It was an old instinct, a throwback to a previous time. After Rosa had left the barrio to study in Manila, such physical contact – contact for the sake of comfort – had no longer seemed appropriate. Even when Doming had died, there had been a barrier between them, the kind of invisible cushion that can exist between two magnets when held a certain way. Usually, it felt to Corazon as if this had been an unspoken agreement – one based on age, on coming of age, leaving home, the shockingly fast transition into adulthood that Rosa had made out of her parents' company. Other times, Corazon felt it was the price she had been made to pay for her child's escape from the barrio and its traps. And other times still, Corazon worried that something else altogether might have happened.

She knew that the last occasion she had been able to touch her daughter, without being *aware* she was touching her daughter, had been during the terrible typhoon. The rainstorm had continued for days, and each night Rosa had gone to sleep in Corazon's arms. Corazon remembered it well. The way that her arms had ached, and how she had often wanted to shift position. Not that she had minded her arms aching. Not that one moment had passed between then and now in which she would not have happily done it again.

But a brushed hand, or similar gesture, was the closest she had come since Rosa had left the barrio and begun her new life in Manila. And, of course, Rosa had left for Manila directly after the rainstorm.

A strange thought, when put like that. Not comfortable, not worth dwelling on.

And anyway, why dwell on the obvious? There was a clear implication: if anything was to blame for the change that had occurred, it was Manila. Manila changed most of the people it touched, so why would her daughter be any different? Nothing to do with coming of age or prices paid. Just the dark city.

As predicted: a brief rinse and the ice-cream bowl was clean, so Corazon wondered what she might do to occupy herself next. Something normal and mundane was called for. If she couldn't surround her daughter in her arms, she could at least surround her with reassuring normality.

Still wondering, Corazon glanced up from the sink and looked out of the window. There she saw clouds of night-time insects, whirling under the downward glow of each street-lamp. An unusual number of them, moving in a graceless slow-motion, as if they were in a dream.

And, equally belonging to a world of dreams, or childhood recollections of skipping-rope chants, she saw a silhouette.

3

Corazon took three or four steps away from the sink, turning as she did so. Rosa scraped her chair backwards. Through the ceiling, there was the soft bump of small feet sliding off their beds and landing on floorboards.

Rosa asked Corazon what she had seen, and Corazon raised a hand to the side of her face. Rosa didn't feel any particular alarm, didn't make any connection with the exchange of gunfire ten minutes earlier, because Corazon's expression was more of puzzlement and surprise than anything else. She was almost smiling. 'I *thought* I saw . . .' she said, but didn't end the sentence.

'Mum!' called Lita.

Rosa looked towards the hallway, then back at her mother. Corazon, still holding the side of her face, still seeming no more than vaguely startled, looked back at the window.

'Mum!'

Lita's voice was clearer, less muffled, coming from the top of the stairs.

Rosa swore. '*Stay* in your room, honey!'

'Are you going to come up?'

'*Yes*,' Rosa replied, not moving. 'I'll be right up. I want you to go *back* in your *room*.'

'I *thought* I saw . . .'

The man outside was on his hands and knees, crouched in the middle of the road. A thick covering of indeterminate filth glistened or glittered on his clothes and body. He had an automatic pistol. His head was hanging loosely and his chest was heaving.

· Suddenly he rolled over, holding his arms out stiffly. The gun swung around so it pointed down the length of his body. He was aiming at the street behind him, where, distinct under the sodium lamps, two more men had appeared.

Hollow be Thy Name

I

In the nine years since she had left the barrio, Rosa made the return journey over the Sierra Madre mountains only five times. While she had been finishing school and starting university, she had made the trip home each Christmas, staying for no more than three days. After meeting Sonny, in her first year as a medical student, she had not returned to the barrio at all. Their marriage, eight months later, had taken place in Batangas – the home of Sonny's family.

Twice a year, Corazon and Doming would make the reverse trip to visit Rosa in Manila. They would stay at Uncle Rey's. The purpose of their trip was twofold. Partly, they missed their daughter – especially Doming, who had never had a clear understanding of the reasons for Rosa's abrupt departure – and partly to petition Uncle Rey for more college funds. Rey was always agreeable to the petition, having been the main reason that Rosa's career had been pointed in the direction of medicine. Usually, he had arranged for the transferral of money several days before Corazon and Doming had even shown up.

If Doming hadn't died, Rosa would never have made the journey for a sixth time. If Doming had lived for ever.

Changes, in the nine years: the sawmill had expanded, exhausted the supply of trees around Infanta, and begun to strip the jungle along the mountain road. The river, visible as the road began its descent towards the coastline, was permanently brown from landslides in the deforested areas. The stretch between Siniloan and Real was tarmacked. On the tarmac were Japanese and Korean saloon cars. Saloon cars hitting thirty or forty miles an hour, where jeepneys – weaving around countless pot-holes and ruts – had once been lucky to touch fifteen.

Just the start of the changes.

Nobody looked up when an engine passed. Nobody hitched rides, because the rides were moving too fast to stop. The horses, which had lived in a glade by a hairpin turn, had vanished. Concrete tubes redirected streams. The journey took two and a half hours less than it used to.

'Different,' said Sonny, accelerating the Honda saloon car to overtake a Kapalaran bus.

'You can't imagine,' Rosa replied.

'All that used to be jungle. This used to be a dirt track. There weren't any power lines.'

'Okay, you can.'

Sonny glanced cautiously at his wife out of the corner of his eyes. 'Caribou munched on fields of wild orchids. Rare birds took fruit out of the hands of children.'

'Mmm.'

'Mammoths would stampede down from the mountain summits . . .'

There was no acknowledgement.

'Rose,' Sonny said, after a brief pause, and reached over the gear stick to squeeze her knee. 'Is there the slightest chance of getting a smile out of you?'

Rosa shook her head, though she gave Sonny's hand a squeeze in return. 'There's no chance. I'm sorry.'

'That's okay,' said Sonny quickly. 'Don't be sorry. I'm just trying to . . .'

'You're trying to make this easier.'

'In any way I can, if you just tell me what to do.'

'There's nothing.'

'But if you realize there is something . . .'

'Yes.'

'You just tell me.'

'I will.'

Raphael, lying on Rosa's lap, head rolling with the turns, stirred. Two months past his first birthday. A better sleeper, at that age, than his older sister had been.

2

Rosa started to feel ill when they reached the coast – which meant that Infanta, and Sarap, were now no more than a thirty-minute drive away. She asked Sonny to pull over, handed him the baby, got out of the car, and threw up. While she was throwing up, Sonny also got out of the car and came to stand behind her. It reminded her of Lito and the dead pig on the beach, and made her throw up again.

'This is too hard for you,' said Sonny. 'We'll drive back to Manila. Tomorrow, I'll collect Corazon myself.'

'No,' said Rosa, over her shoulder. 'I'm not missing my father's funeral. Just give me a few minutes on my own. I'll be fine.'

A short walk took her down a grassy slope and on to sand. Feeling the eyes of her husband and children – watching her from the Honda – she manoeuvred herself until the car's bright-blue paint was obscured by road-side trees and bushes. Then she sat down, half-way between the high-tide watermark and the sea itself.

'Your beauty is as rare as your fingerprint.'

It was an unexpected line, said earnestly and with a noticeably prepared seriousness. Thinking back on it, many times, Rosa suspected that Lito had lifted the line from a Sari-Sari store romance comic. She also suspected that the next line would have been a proposal for marriage. Which, if her life had been her own, she would have accepted.

But instead, she had told him that within forty-eight hours she was going to be on a jeepney headed for Manila, where she would live with her Uncle Rey. And she had told him that they would probably never see each other again.

Lito said that he didn't believe her. He had a look on his face as if he'd just staggered out of the sea with bleeding ears and glass splinters peppered in his skin. Rosa thought maybe she had the same look on her face. She certainly had it in her head. When she screamed at Lito, telling him that it was true, she felt as if she were screaming through cotton wool. And when the words came out, they were whispered.

Lito asked why. Why Manila, why never seeing each other again. Rosa had answered him in kind, by lunging forwards and hitting him. Or scratching him. On the chest.

It was hard to remember the specifics, in the same way that it was hard to remember why her answer had taken the form of an assault. Except that it was appropriate. Without fairness or reason – appropriate in its context.

Then she was pulled back by Doming, who must have followed her when she had run out of the house early that morning, tracking her, noiseless as the world which he had come to inhabit. Doming, who had not understood the silent-movie scene that had exploded in front of him the night before – Corazon and Rosa twisting their mouths into inexplicable expressions of fury and hatred – but who had understood its aftermath well enough. Saw it on his daughter's face as she had seen it on his face, as she had seen it on Lito's face. And indeed, as Doming could see it on Lito's face.

This boy with a strangely ruined chest, reeling under the dynamite shock. Son of Tata Vin, the man with the strangely ruined leg. Withered like a polio victim – the fingers of one hand could have closed around Tata Vin's thigh. But at least Tata Vin had been better off than *his* father. Tata Vin's father had been born without any arms below the elbow. It made you wonder what a family could have done to be so cursed.

Perhaps three hundred metres down the beach, Doming stopped and sat down. He still held Rosa, managing to contain her rage with one entirely powerful arm, while the other was kept free to stroke her head. It took time for her red mist and wild-cat strength to dissolve, but eventually it did.

When he released her, he checked Rosa's eyes for the autopilot. And when he found it – found the blankness – he relaxed, partially, because he knew that whatever the nature of this explosion, the autopilot would guide her through.

3

Doming was in an open casket. A good casket, white with brass handles and gold-plated edging, and a Perspex viewing window. It had been paid for largely by Sonny, who – while Rosa was still a trainee doctor – was the family's only real earner. He was congratulated by several of the mourners for having honoured his father-in-law with such a lavish send-off.

'I doubt I'd have done the same for my father-in-law,' whispered Turing, who already had a few San Miguels under his belt. And it was quite a belt. The spread of his girth had been so extreme that Rosa hadn't been able to place him at first. 'Turing,' he had prompted cheerfully. 'I might not have married Leesha if I'd known she was such a good cook!'

Recognizing Leesha, however, was no problem. Of course she looked older, and three children had added a complementing weight to her, but in all other aspects she was the same. And anyway, in the five intervening years between Rosa's last trip to Sarap, the two of them had exchanged photos – Leesha's presumably taken by the ballooning Turing, his expansion hidden behind the camera.

And Rosa recognized Ella easily too. Where Leesha had glided, Ella had scuttled, tugging after her a thin man with a greasy, translucent complexion, and a slightly haunted air.

'My deepest condolences,' she had said. 'Everyone will miss your father.'

Knowing better than to open her mouth, for fear of what might come out, Rosa simply nodded. Then she turned away, to where Leesha was showering a somewhat bemused Lita with kisses and hugs. Ella and her husband left not long after.

Late into the night, at around twelve, the very oldest and the very youngest at the wake had drifted home, been taken home, or were curled up asleep in the house. Everyone else was outside. The teenagers were sitting in a circle around an oil-lamp, taking turns singing recent pop songs. Relatively recent. Rosa noticed that there was still a detectable time-lag between Manila and the barrio.

Sonny was in another circle – a circle of husbands. He had been roped into a lambanog drinking session, organized by Turing. Unused to the locally distilled spirit, he had discovered that he had got himself extremely drunk, but far too late to do anything about it.

Corazon was on her own, with the coffin, one hand laid on the Perspex. She had been there since Rosa had arrived, as she would be until the casket was taken to the church the next day.

And Rosa and Leesha sat together, separate from the others, having the private chat they had been waiting for all evening.

'Now,' said Leesha, pouring herself a shot from her own supply of lambanog. 'Do you want to talk about how you feel?'

'I don't think so. I'd rather hear about you. You know, you look so good, and all your children are beautiful.'

'Thank you. I agree. I wish I could say the same about my man, though. Your photos of Sonny don't do him justice, whereas perhaps you've noticed that Turing's photos . . .'

'I haven't seen photos of Turing. You didn't send me any.'

'Exactly. I didn't send you any pictures of a caribou's arse either.'

'Leesha!'

'Just a joke.'

'There aren't . . . problems between you?'

'None at all. Everything's fine. I'm very happily married, and I'm sure it's going to stay that way.'

'I'm glad to hear it.'

'Although I must admit, I have my doubts about the third baby. She's a girl, so I'm hoping that if my doubts are confirmed, it won't show up too much. But if it had been a boy . . . well, it doesn't bear thinking about.'

Rosa frowned, turning this comment over in her mind. Then she said, 'Oh.'

'Sison,' said Leesha, probably a little louder than she should have, and knocked back her shot. 'Don't look at me like that. I held back for *four* years. But it seemed like everywhere I looked, there he was, playing basketball, being handsome. It drove me crazy.'

So it turned out that Rosa had been wrong, because she managed a smile after all.

*

They never talked about Lito. At one point, Rosa had been tempted to ask. From Leesha's letters, Rosa knew that he was still a fisherman, and that he was still unmarried. But now that Rosa and Leesha were face to face, talking about him didn't seem easy.

Rosa had almost wanted him to appear at the wake. Even if they didn't speak, just to see him, she thought, would tell her what she needed to know. If he was okay. If he'd moved on in the way that she had.

To the extent that she had.

Guilty towards Sonny that she was thinking about Lito so much, guilty towards her father that Lito was the biggest reason why this return to Sarap was so hard.

Perhaps he would appear at the funeral tomorrow. Perhaps, if he did, that would be a good thing.

4

Leesha stayed the night with Rosa and the children, behind the curtain partition that had once made Rosa's bedroom. Raphael lay in the protective arc formed by Rosa's right arm. Lita lay similarly with Leesha, though she was too big to be completely encircled, so Leesha's arm doubled as a pillow.

It left no space for Sonny, but by the time he realized how important it was for him to stop drinking and get some shut-eye, he was far beyond caring where that shut-eye might happen to be found. He woke at five the next morning, hung over and still extremely drunk, puzzled to discover Corazon's toes only a few inches from his face. Puzzled, then appalled, when he discovered that his search for a bed had led him under the trestles that supported Doming's coffin.

Which partly explained the fitful dream that had plagued him for each of the three hours he had been approximating sleep. His own death, repeatedly, by a variety of means, but always at the hands of the fat sawmill guy with the sadistic drinking games. 'Just one more!' Turing would cry, pulling a *byenté nwébe* from his back pocket. 'Just one more!' as he started stabbing Sonny in the neck. 'No,' Sonny would protest politely. 'Really, I think I've had enough.' 'Just one more!' And the next time, it would be a gun, or a machete.

Coincidentally, Leesha had also dreamed of Turing. She was playing a game of one-on-one basketball with Sison, and the ball was Turing's head.

'Corazon, I am *so* sorry. Please forgive me, *po*,' Sonny tried to say as he crawled out from beneath the coffin, but his lips were dry and stuck together, and didn't open. Fortunately, Corazon was too exhausted to take much notice of the bizarre, sing-song whine that came from her son-in-law's nose.

Sonny hauled himself up, desperately trying to produce saliva and massage some life into his mouth with his tongue. Once he'd pulled the creases out of his shirt and regained some dignity, he made a second go of the apology.

'I don't know what to say, *po* . . . There's nothing I *can* say. I am *so* sorry.'

'Oh, Sonny,' Corazon replied, gazing at him through bleary and bloodshot eyes. 'I'm sorry too. I don't know what I'll do without him. But I know he is with Jesus now. He was a good man all his life, a *good* man, and I know he is with Jesus.'

Sonny blinked at her.

'And I want you to know that I was touched you spent the night keeping me company. You can be sure, I won't forget it.'

'It . . . was . . . the least I could do.'

'It is a great source of happiness to me that my daughter has

134

been blessed with such a husband. You are a very fine young man.'

'Thank you,' Sonny said, as his brain struggled with its toxicity, attempting to keep pace with this endlessly twisting situation. 'And you are a very fine old woman.'

Corazon's bleary eyes widened. 'Excuse me?'

'I said . . . I need some water.'

' . . . Did you?'

'No,' Sonny replied – firmly, to compensate for the long hesitation. 'I didn't.' Then he blinked again. 'About this water.'

' . . . It's over there, in the clay pot.'

'Ah, yes,' he said, resting a light hand on the coffin to prevent himself from falling over. 'So it is.'

'You are a very fine old woman,' he was still muttering to himself, an hour later, sobered up on sugary black coffee and the morning air. 'What was I *thinking* of?'

While Leesha and Lita continued to sleep, Rosa suckled the baby and – through a slit in the nipa – watched Sonny walking around the vegetable garden. Every few steps he would visibly shudder, or tap aggressively at his temples.

Rosa had no idea what lay behind his odd behaviour, but she didn't particularly care. Her dreams had been as vivid and circular as Sonny's, and as unfaithful as Leesha's, though nothing like as coded. She was simply relieved that, on waking, she could look at her husband and feel sure that she loved him.

5

The long walk to the church and the long service inside passed in a blur of non-thinking for Rosa. All morning, her mind was distracted by the smallest things. The yellowness of the dust on her black cotton dress. The length of Lita's stride compared to her own (the ratio was almost exactly two steps to one). The drone in the priest's voice that made it impossible to follow what he was saying.

In fact, until the funeral procession had left the church and reached the graveyard, it was the priest who had provoked Rosa's strongest emotional response. Watching him – this fleshy, closeted, virginal man who had gone out of his way to experience as little of life as possible – Rosa felt a surge of irritation. It seemed absurd that such a lifeless person should be called upon to clarify the end of someone else's. 'I knew Tata Doming well,' he intoned, and Rosa had to stop herself from interrupting his address. 'Oh, shut up,' she imagined herself saying. 'You don't know anything well, let alone any*body*.' The urge caught her off guard and made her blush, afraid that her thoughts had somehow been loud enough to be heard by the mourners in the surrounding pews. And perhaps they had been. Without warning, Raphael started wailing loudly and fighting Rosa's hold. Sonny gestured to pass the baby over, but instead Rosa took it as an opportunity to excuse herself from the service.

'He's probably hungry, and he's too hot in here,' she whispered as she eased past Sonny and Corazon, perfectly aware that these were not hungry or uncomfortable tears. Corazon probably knew too, but if she disapproved of Rosa's exit, she didn't show it. Instead she nodded, and gave her daughter a vaguely awkward – but sympathetic – pat on the back of the leg.

*

It was while Rosa was sitting in the café opposite the church, with the now-docile Raphael chewing idly on a drinking straw, that she saw Lito.

She was about twenty metres away from where he stood, sitting at a table in the shadow cast by the café's canvas awning. He was amazed by how much of her was so entirely familiar. Not just her features, build, posture – her mannerisms. When she tilted her head, he knew exactly how far her head would tilt. He could read the exact nature of the movement. He knew she was squinting at the sunshine and the bright road beneath his feet, and he knew that he was as recognizable to her as she had been to him. And he knew she was pleased to see him, even before she jumped up and began to run across the road.

Knew he could stop her, dead in her tracks, with a raised hand.

Knew *everything*.

It terrified him.

Knew, that when he turned to go, she wouldn't follow.

The years that had changed nothing, the child in her arms, her eyes on his back, the ache in his chest, the bottle in his hands.

Small green bottle.

Terrified him.

6

Terrified her.

One look, she had thought, would tell her what she needed to know. If he'd moved on in the way she had; if he was okay. And she had been right, because one look had been enough. He wasn't okay at all.

'I'm not having *grandchildren* with *bits* of them *missing*!' Corazon had once screamed over the tail-end of a typhoon.

Seeing Lito now, it was more than a part of his anatomy that was missing. Apparent in the shadow that had stood in the sunlight, radiating blankness: his anatomy had been vacated. *He* was missing.

When the priest's interminable service drew to a close, and the mourners began to file out of the church, they found Rosa in the same place she had been stopped by Lito's raised hand. Raphael's hair was plastered over his head with sweat, and his breathing was heavy. When Sonny tried to take the baby from her, Rosa's arms felt like iron and didn't give an inch.

'What is it?' he said, hating the stupidity of such a question at a funeral, feeling helpless. When Rosa didn't answer, he almost tried to take the baby again, but decided against it when he saw her frozen expression. He had been frightened away, if he was honest with himself.

Half a decade later, fixing a tyre, he would tell Raphael that it wasn't God who had burned his chest. Sonny would never let God take responsibilty for that moment of cowardice.

7

For Raphael, there would be a chain of events that would take many years to fully explain. Certain details would be held back, according to suitability of age. In its incomplete form, the chain of events took the form of a sad story about a jealous man. But in time, he would come to think of himself as a boy with two histories: one biological, and the other anatomical. One with a nine-month gap between conception and birth, and the other with a gap of nine years. Ultimately, a boy with two fathers.

Doming died at the gates of the graveyard. Everywhere else – the house, the road to the church, the church itself – he had been alive. In the same way that nobody is about to leave until they reach the bus depot and see the bus: alive. And characteristically quiet.

But at the gates of the graveyard he died, suddenly, and Rosa was overwhelmed by the understanding. She burst into tears. They streamed down her face as the procession walked on the stone pathways between the tombs, and when the seal of the miniature family mausoleum was broken open, she started to sob.

This, Sonny felt, was acceptable for Lita to see. Her mother's sorrow obviously distressed the little girl. But witnessing the grief seemed important, as much about life as death, and his instincts told him he shouldn't hide her from it.

When Doming's body was removed from the coffin to be slid into the tomb, however, he changed his mind. It wasn't the corpse. It was that Rosa, with Corazon, became hysterical.

Sonny felt he had three priorities: to deal with Lita, then Raphael, then Rosa, in that order. Lita first, because she happened to be with him. He would take her back out of the crowd, as far away from the shrieking as possible, and give her to one of the people he recognized from the night before. Hopefully Leesha. Back into the crowd to grab Raphael, whether Rosa was willing to give him up or not. And back again for Rosa, whom he would simply hold.

In none of this was politeness a priority, and Sonny made his route through Doming's relatives, neighbours and friends with force. Their reluctance to step aside was confusing, but not a concern. If they didn't step aside, they were pushed.

Once out, he called Leesha's name. But Turing appeared instead, wordlessly scooping up Lita in one arm, and pushing on Sonny's shoulders to propel him back into the crowd. For that, his memory of Turing would always be accompanied by a rush of undiluted affection. A rush he had felt at the time, equally undiluted, and an important memory to retain. Part of the truth, the concentration of events, the contradictions that sat side by side.

It was a voice, Rosa would tell Raphael, that cut through her hysteria and made itself heard. She didn't think about why the voice could do this so easily. She did what the voice told her to do.

'The baby. Give him to me.'

Perhaps half a minute later, Raphael's cry filled Sonny with pain. A grip like gravity, a horror like the surface of the sun, a suck like a rip tide – it effortlessly and continuously transcended itself. It marked something terrible.

More memories to sit side by side, the mystery of the crowd. Sonny's path was *still* blocked by people who were reluctant to move aside.

Sonny punched them until they fell. Harder, flatter fist, no restraint, when he saw their faces. With Raphael's cries driving him insane, their stunned outrage was a lifeline to the comprehensible.

8

Sonny saw the fiercely smoking bundle laid out on the ground, and thought his baby was on fire. But tearing at Raphael's clothes, he found no fire. Yet the baby *was* burning, and his own hands were now burning too.

Then he felt the *manner* in which they were burning, and realized that the smoke was from acid. The burning was chemical, not as penetrating as heat. Aggressive, like tear-gas in Rizal Park from his undergraduate days.

'Water,' he shouted at the static circle of people around him. They stared back, indignant and mute, holding their bruises.

If only there *had* been flames. He could have smothered flames. Instead of pawing uselessly at an invisible corrosive liquid, he would have been able to *do* something.

'God, help me,' he screamed.

Able to do nothing, nothing would stop the acid from burning though his baby's tiny chest and delicate ribs. The acid would burn through to its heart.

'Help me!'

Raphael stopped crying and started gasping. Between Sonny's own cries were pockets of numb silence.

'*Somebody*, get some *water*!'

The third time he shouted it, somebody did: a young man, dressed unusually for a funeral – ragged shorts, sandals and a bright-white T-shirt. He pulled a bucket of water from behind a tombstone, as if a bucket was always kept there in event of acid attack. He walked over, calm and unrushed, but with an air of pragmatic concentration. Sonny might have imagined that he was a doctor approaching with a briefcase. In this way, the young man made Sonny think of his wife.

He made Sonny feel as if he didn't exist. He squatted down beside Raphael, and Sonny was excluded. First relegated to position of watcher, then erased.

Cupping water from the bucket, pouring it over the baby,

using the pads of his thumbs to rub at the baby's skin. Talking to the baby. In his soft Quezon accent, the young man was saying, 'There, there.'

As he poured more water: 'There, there, little guy. There, there, sunshine. You're okay now.'

Almost cooing, bent over as if he was doing little more than gazing into a cot.

'Dad's here.'

Sonny saw the small green bottle, stuck into the waistband of the young man's shorts. He had obviously thrust it there in a hurry, because the cap hadn't been twisted properly and a single drip had escaped. It had run down the bottle neck, and had begun eating into the shorts material. Eating like a pinprick of light eats a dry leaf under a magnifying glass.

Sonny thought about the ready bucket of water behind the tombstone, and gave up trying to make sense of the senseless.

He was pulled off Lito by several of the other mourners, none of whom had the slightest idea what was going on. But they had been given enough pause to be snapped out of their previous passive stupor. And though Sonny was a stranger to all of them, they knew that he was obviously a violent man, given to lashing out at whoever was close to hand, and that it would be best if he were contained before his violence got out of control.

9

Sense from the senseless. The weeks following the funeral passed, and Rosa spoke more, and Raphael began healing – as much as he ever would. And, as much as he ever would, Sonny reached a point of understanding.

When it happened, he said in all seriousness, 'I'm going to kill him. That sick fucker. I'm going to go back to Sarap and kill him.'

Rosa, who saw Sonny's understanding only in terms of its limits, kept her reply precise, honest and unelaborated. 'Sonny, if you hurt Lito in any way, at any time, I will stop loving you. You will lose me and never get me back.'

So Sonny left Lito alone, because he believed her. These are the things, he decided, that we learn we can live with.

The Conquistador Closes His Eyes

Too confused to have understood their mother's shouts, Raphael and Lita had crept down the stairs and were huddled in the hallway. They stood half-way between the kitchen and the sitting room, pressed to the frayed Last Supper wall hanging. Through the kitchen doorway, they could see where Corazon lay dying. Her arms were bent over her ears, and her legs were bunched up to her body. She had pulled them there a few moments before being shot, to shield herself from the broken glass that had skidded across the floor.

Rosa was a shield. Behind her was the man who had jumped through the window. He tumbled over the sink and scrabbled on the linoleum. Pushed around on the linoleum with his bleeding hands. Slipped on his blood and the glass that had showered around him. Glittered with the glass and the wet black filth on his clothes and skin. Then he had leapt up to grab Rosa and drag her towards him.

Rosa was the shield, dragged and held to protect this blackened glittering man from the two other men who were hiding outside. She had seen them briefly through the window's frame, running from the road towards the house. They had ducked out of view as a bullet ripped over their heads. And they had shot back through the window, missing the dark man entirely and hitting Corazon instead.

*

'I don't know who you are,' said Rosa. 'But I want you to let me go, and get out of my house.'

The man squeezed her tighter. He was trembling. She could feel his jaw on her shoulder, and she could feel his stubble on her neck.

'My mother is dying. You are putting my children in danger.'

His teeth were clicking in her ear.

'Let me go and run now, before they shoot again. Run down the hall.'

'Ah,' said the man. And spoke in English. '*Jesus fucking Christ. I'm dead.*'

'*Let me go now, and run down the hall. Leave through the doorway at the end. You can escape.*'

'*Dead,*' said the man again. He panted, and growled.

3—2

Black Dog is Here

I

Behind the colourful oil-slick on the puddle's surface, a monochrome face gazed cautiously back at itself. A face that became increasingly troubled, screwing up its young features into an expression of disappointment and dismay.

Dust, thought Vincente. Although he'd suspected he was dirty, his reflection had still come as a shock. Usually he managed to keep clean, but there hadn't been any rain for at least a week and the daytime heat was dry, so there was a lot of dust blowing around the streets.

'Boom!' he added out loud a few moments later. The night before, he had been caught in Rizal Park by a Barangay Tanod patrol, and they had given him a haircut. A hygiene haircut, they described it, intended to prevent lice infestation in street-kid communities. A punishment haircut to anyone else. Clippers wielded fiercely by a fat hand, leaving a bruised and bleeding scalp, with unshaved patches of little tufts and curls. The little tufts stood bolt upright. It looked to Vincente as if his head had been frozen in mid-comic-book explosion. Even more so when he raised his eyebrows and opened his mouth into an O of exploding surprise, and said 'Boom'. And even more yet when he shifted position so that the sun was also reflected in the puddle, burning red around him like a devil's halo. A hard bullet of spit impressively completed the effect. Vincente broke apart into ripples and shrapnel light.

Then he stood up. Red sun wouldn't see out the next half-hour. Before that happened, he wanted to get to Ermita, track down Totoy, and get some kind of plan together for the approaching night.

2

Unlike his friend Vincente, Totoy was small for a thirteen-year-old. Or, to be more accurate, both Vincente and Totoy were small for their age – the result of a poor diet, according to the Irish priest who ran the Roxas soup kitchen – but Vincente was less small. That made Totoy absolutely tiny. He could easily have passed for an eight-year-old, should he have ever wanted to, and other kids frequently made him the butt of sizeist jokes.

'Hey, Totoy, I've got an earache. You want to creep in and take a look?'

Even his mother, who he sometimes saw around the bus terminal, dragging around a comatose baby or two, usually greeted him by saying, 'Still as small as ever, I see.'

For this reason, if he had nothing better to do, Totoy liked to stand on walls. He felt that the world was a more interesting place when viewed from the higher perspective.

'Get off the wall, kiddo,' said the blue-uniformed security guard outside the Ermita McDonald's. He waved his stockless shotgun in Totoy's general direction. 'You can't stand there.'

Totoy hesitated before turning to face the guard. This wall was a particularly good one, giving a view directly into the bright restaurant windows and its hypnotically clean interior. 'Can't stand here, *po*? he said. 'Why the fuck not?'

The guard smiled. 'You're way too young for that tongue, kiddo. Come on, down you get.'

Totoy hesitated again, this time because the doors to the restaurant had been swung open, releasing a gust of the unique McDonald's smell. A good smell, as alluring and mysterious as a rich lady's perfume. All the more mysterious because it was strikingly unreminiscent of any other food Totoy could think of. 'Why can't I stand here?' he rephrased more politely, once he had breathed in his fill.

'I have to tell you?'

'I'm not doing anything wrong. Not begging or hassling the customers. I haven't even got my hand out.'

'You're bringing down the tone.'

'Tone?'

'We have a tone to keep up here.'

'All I'm doing is standing on a wall.'

'A McDonald's wall. Private property, kiddo.'

'I see.' Totoy put his hands on his hips. 'And are you going to shoot me, *po*? If I don't get down, you going to shoot me?'

'Sure.'

'Really?'

'Well.' The guard pushed back the peak of his cap. 'No. But I might set the clown on you.'

' . . . What's the clown going to do?'

'Turn you into a hamburger and sell you in a bun.'

Made sense: skin that white, teeth that long. Glancing at one of the posters, it seemed unlikely that lipstick could make a grin so broad or crimson. 'Might turn me into a Big Mac,' said Totoy thoughtfully.

'Might.'

'Okay.' He took a last look around him and jumped down. 'I'm off your stupid wall, *po*. You keep that clown away from me.'

The guard nodded. 'Deal, kiddo,' he said.

3

Vincente made his way down Roxas Boulevard by keeping to the central island or weaving through the cars. It was probably slower than using the pavement, but habit kept him to the tarmac. Despite wanting to track down Totoy before nightfall, he was keeping half an eye open for drivers who looked like they might be a soft touch. Parents mainly, with kids in the back seat, or anyone in a taxi.

Habit, even though begging from the traffic jams was hardly worth the effort these days. Increasingly, most cars had air-con, so their windows were always up. And the windows were tinted, so you couldn't make the eye contact, and you almost invariably needed eye contact if you were going to score some money. Air-con and, particularly, tinted windows were a curse. Their shadowed mirrors gave the unwelcome impression that you were begging from a darker version of yourself.

Sure enough, by the time Vincente had reached Legaspi Towers – where he turned left off the boulevard – he had made precisely one peso. And that peso hadn't even come as a single score, but as two separate fifty-centavo pieces, from two separate cheapskate drivers. Ironic, he commented to himself, that the traffic jams had become less rewarding, given that they were heavier and slower-moving than they had ever been before.

Luckily he was given a chance to supplement his poor takings when, sitting on the steps of the side entrance to Legaspi Towers, he saw Alfredo. Vincente glanced at the skies and estimated he had quarter of an hour in hand before it became imperative that he find Totoy. Cutting it fine, he decided, but doable, as long as he didn't get involved in one of Alfredo's long chats.

Alfredo was reading, peering at the words through round glasses, hunched over so that his slim body almost made a circle. He was always reading. With his street-kid clients, the popular belief was that he was searching for an elusive gap that existed somewhere in his books, hidden between lines or letters. One that would allow him, once and for all, to crawl inside the pages and disappear.

'Hey, Fredo.'

Alfredo didn't answer, making Vincente wait impatiently while he finished his paragraph. 'Hi, Cente,' he eventually said, and carefully laid the book beside him.

'What's up?'

'Not much. See you've met the Barangay Tanod.'

'Huh?' Vincente ran his fingers over his patchy scalp. 'Nope, I did this myself.'

'Yourself?'

'Yep. It's all the rage. You'll be seeing a lot of it soon, among the fashionable circles.'

'All the rage . . .' Alfredo chuckled and rearranged his glasses in a way that made him look older than his twenty-eight years. 'I don't know whether to believe you or not. It might be true for all I know.'

'It isn't,' said Vincente. 'I was joking. Now listen, I've got a dream for you.'

'A dream? Sorry, but it isn't your day today. You aren't till the day after tomorrow.'

'I'm short of cash.'

'Come on, Cente. You know I have to keep a strict weekly rotation. It isn't fair on the other kids.'

'My dreams are the best.'

'They are,' said Alfredo reluctantly. 'Interesting, and well remembered . . .'

'So?'

'So, I do already have Totoy's dream today . . . but . . .' Alfredo waved a hand. 'That boy is useless. All he dreams about is guns and girls, and fighting battles in which he is the hero. And, needless to say, they aren't even his real dreams. They're his fantasies.'

'Really,' said Vincente, without interest. He had often heard this complaint before.

'Of course, that has some interest too. Seeing what he chooses to make his fantasies . . . but they're always the same. Gangster dreams, war dreams, dreams with aliens in outer space. If there was some variety, I wouldn't mind so much.'

'To be honest, Fredo,' Vincente interrupted, 'I'm in a bit of a hurry, so do you want the dream or not?'

'I'm not sure,' said Alfredo. 'I have Totoy's dream . . .' But his hand was already reaching for the Sony tape recorder he kept in his knapsack. 'Oh, what the hell. Go on, then. Let's hear it.'

'Good decision,' said Vincente. 'You'll like this one.'

The tape recorder clicked on.

'Okay. So I was standing by a sink . . .'

I was standing by a white stone sink in a kitchen, which I thought was the kitchen of my old home. I'm not sure, because of my memory. Then my father walks in from outside – it's a hot day outside, because I can see through the doorway – and he says, look at this. I look, and in his hand he's holding the most tiny baby you could imagine, probably no more than three or four inches long. I think to myself that the baby is so tiny that you ought to be delicate while handling it, and that my father seems to be handling it carelessly.

The next moment, my father drops the baby. It falls in the sink and slips down the plug-hole. I'm very worried, and my father is panicking slightly, but he isn't actually doing anything. He suggests that he goes to a neighbour to get help — or something like that. But I'm thinking, no, that will take too long because the baby will drown. I know that water always collects in the bent pipe under the sink, and that the baby will be stuck there.

I reach under the sink and yank at the pipe hard and it comes away easily. The baby pops out on to my palm, but it isn't breathing and its mouth is filled with white fluid like baby sick.

I try to revive it by pushing on its stomach very gently and blowing in its mouth. I am very nervous about crushing it. The baby starts breathing again, and I am very relieved, but then it stops breathing again. I revive it again, and it breathes for a few seconds, then stops breathing again.

This keeps happening, and each time I revive it, the baby seems to be in worse pain. It's trying to cry and wriggle. By now, I know for sure that it is dying and I won't be able to save it. But I don't seem to be able to stop myself from trying, even though I know there is no hope and I am only causing the baby extra pain.

That's where it ends. I wake up.

' . . . Have you ever seen a foetus?'

'What's a foetus?'

'A foetus . . .' Alfredo paused. 'Similar to what you described. A very tiny baby. Maybe your mother or a sister might have been pregnant and lost the baby inside. Did you ever see anything like that?'

Vincente shook his head. 'Not as far as I know. But, I can't remember them too well, so . . . Maybe.'

'How do you know how to resuscitate someone? Pushing on the chest, blowing in the mouth . . .'

'Seen it.'

'Did the dream feel like a nightmare?'

'Sure.'

'You woke up feeling . . .?'

'Bad.'

'And what do you think the dream might mean?'

Vincente laughed. 'I know what *you* think it might mean.'

'Go on.'

'You think the baby is me, and I'm angry with my father for disappearing when I was so young. Or maybe you think the baby is Totoy, because I look after him sometimes.'

'Mmm . . .'

'But you are also interested in the sink. You've noticed I said it was stone, and there was plumbing, so you are wondering what that says about my upbringing. And my memory.'

'Yes.' Alfredo nodded. 'You are absolutely correct. And as usual, your perceptiveness has confounded all my expectations, no matter how often I revise them.' Then he leaned forwards and stared straight into Vincent's eyes. 'I should be used to it by now, Cente, but I'm not. I can never predict what's going to come out of your mouth. You're an endless surprise.'

'You always say that.'

'Well, what do you want me to say? You always surprise me.'

'Give me my money, please.'

'Exactly,' Alfredo said delightedly, switching off his tape machine and reaching into his pocket for some change. 'QED.'

4

From his new vantage point – perched on the bamboo scaffold outside what had been a pool hall, until it was bought by developers a few months ago – Totoy spotted Vincente jogging towards him. Gleefully, Totoy realized that as long as Vincente didn't cross the road, he would pass directly under the scaffold, which meant he could be leapt upon from above and surprised. One of the advantages of being small was that leaping on people wasn't too dangerous for his victims.

Not that he did it very often. Vincente was practically the only person who could be relied upon to take the surprise with good grace. He might say, 'You know, you're going to have to be careful doing that. One day you'll be too big, and you'll break my neck.' But that would be the extent of the disapproval. And anyway, Totoy suspected it wasn't disapproval so much as a reassurance that his size was only a temporary condition.

Vincente, for his part, had seen Totoy as soon as he had rounded the corner of Nestor Redondo Avenue. He was well used to scanning for Totoy on walls, trees and lamp-posts, and the quick silhouette on the scaffold had not been difficult to identify.

It had, however, left him with a small dilemma. The first level of planks were a good six feet off the ground, which seemed high enough for the ambush to involve a potentially painful velocity. On the other hand, there was Totoy's disappointment to consider, and the whole issue of friendship.

There were no solid facts, only clues.

Vincente had arrived in Manila around five years ago, on an air-conditioned Kapalaran bus. He had been with his father. He didn't understand why the two of them had left their home in Batangas to come to Manila, as nobody had explained it to him. Neither did he expect that he would ever understand. Quite soon after arriving in the city, perhaps within twenty-four hours, his father had vanished.

Like everything from that time, the circumstances and memory of the vanishing were vague. Some time during the morning, or afternoon, his father had bought him a soda and told him to wait near some traffic-lights while he went off to do something. Hours passed and his father didn't return. By the time night rolled around, he had become a street kid.

The clues. Air-conditioned buses were more expensive than non-air-conditioned buses, so it didn't seem likely that he had been brought to Manila to be deliberately abandoned. His recollections of home life were happy and perfectly comfortable. Indeed, above averagely comfortable. Their house had been on the outskirts of a town, made of concrete, and two storeys high. They had a colour television, metal mosquito-netting on the windows, and a carpet in one of the rooms.

So it was unlikely that the abandonment had been the result of financial trouble, as was the case with some of the other kids around. But it was also unlikely that the abandonment had been the result of a lack of love. Within Vincente's recollections were several images of his parents hugging him, kissing him, and being generally affectionate.

Nowhere within Vincente's recollection was the name of his home town, barrio or surname. Alfredo told him that he might have lost these biographical details as a consequence of the trauma of losing his family, although he admitted he wasn't one hundred per cent sure. Alfredo was more sure about Vincente's period as a mute, which he said was *certainly* a consequence of the trauma, and a not uncommon consequence at that.

The reason Vincente's self-imposed silence hadn't continued indefinitely had been Totoy. At the time he met Totoy, he hadn't spoken to anyone for at least a year. Then, walking near the Intramuros ruins one evening, he had paused to lean against a tree. The rustling in the branches alerted his attention, but not enough to make him check the source of the noise. So he never saw the tiny figure in the leaves, lining up its target, preparing to pounce from above.

*

Beneath the bamboo scaffold, Vincente lay on his back, knees bunched up, too winded to do anything but gasp. Totoy sat to his side, waiting for him to get the breath to talk. But when Vincente's breathing had returned to normal, he still hadn't said anything. He just remained on the pavement, staring up at the sky.

'Maybe I'm getting too big for jumping,' Totoy prompted, disconcerted by the silence. 'What do you think, Cente? Do you think I'm getting too big for it?'

Vincente's mouth stayed shut.

'Maybe I shouldn't do it any more,' he continued, his anxiety increasing. 'In case I break your neck.' He lifted his T-shirt and looked down at his taut stomach. 'I could be putting on weight. Maybe I'm too big and heavy these days. What do you think, Cente? . . . Cente!' he added in final frustration. 'Say something!'

'Okay,' Vincente said. 'What do you want to do tonight?'

The Reason of Sleep

I

'—ecording yet?'

'Yes. It's on.'

'So I'll start.'

'Yes. Start.'

'Right. So. I was standing on a street, and I heard a girl crying for help, so I picked up my . . .'

'Stop.'

' . . . Huh?'

'Gun.'

'What?'

'Gun. You heard a girl crying for help, so you picked up your gun and rescued her.'

' . . . It wasn't a gun. I didn't say it was a gun.'

'You were going to.'

'No . . . I wasn't.'

'A knife then. Or a machete.'

'No . . .'

'A club.'

'No! Shut the fuck up, Fredo. Do you want me to tell you or not?'

'Go on, then.'

'Right. I picked up my . . .'

'Axe.'

'No.'

'Bomb?'

160

'No! It wasn't any kind of weapon! It was a . . . bag.'

'A bag. And, only so that we can cut to the chase, what was in the bag?'

'. . . A gun.'

'Okay. Enough.'

'I haven't finished.'

'Yes you have. I don't need this dream. I've got twenty others from you, just like it. Totoy, please try to understand. I'm not really interested in your fantasies. I don't want your day-dreams. I want your night dreams.'

'That was a night dream!'

'No it wasn't.'

'How do you know?'

'Because I can tell. Because of the way it sounds.'

'Yes, well, that's where you're wrong, because actually it was a night dream. I had it at night.'

'But. Were you asleep.'

'You didn't say anything about being asleep. You said day and night.'

'Totoy, you're being wilfully difficult. We've been through this enough times for you to know exactly what I mean. Sleeping dreams. That's what I pay you for.'

'Mmm . . .'

'Look, let's try something else. Why do you think it is that you don't like telling me your sleeping dreams? Is it because you don't think they're very interesting? Maybe you think that your waking dreams are more exciting.'

'My waking dreams are very exciting, it's true.'

'Or maybe it's because there's something about your sleeping dreams that you don't think you should share. Are your sleeping dreams frightening? Perhaps you don't tell me them because you don't want to remember. Or because you can't remember . . .'

'You know, Fredo, I've got an upset stomach.'

'. . . *What?*'

'*I've got an upset stomach. I've had it for days. I've thrown up a couple of times, but mainly I've got the shits.*'

'*Oh . . . well . . . do you want some medicine? If you come back when I get off work, we could go to a chemist.*'

'*No thanks. But I have to go now. My stomach feels bad. I'd better go.*'

'. . . *Okay.*'

'*Can I have the money, please.*'

'. . . *Sure, Totoy. Just let me switch off the machi—*'

2

Alfredo hit the stop button on the Walkman and took off his headphones. Then he massaged his temples as if he were easing away a nagging headache. There was no headache, but he felt as if there should have been. Of the seven kids he regularly interviewed, Totoy was the one he most associated with headaches.

Totoy was so unlike Cente.

Alfredo stuffed his Walkman into his knapsack and stood up. Looking around, he was disoriented by the darkness. The last time he had looked around, registered his surroundings, it had been to talk to Vincente. Then, Roxas Boulevard and the water in Manila Bay had been burning with a beautiful orange light.

'Light from the sun,' Alfredo muttered.

A passer-by on the pavement stopped and turned, thinking he was being addressed. It took him a moment to realize that he wasn't, and that the slight man on the steps of Legaspi Towers was talking to himself. Or to the black sky, which was the direction his head was pointed.

'Light from our nearest star, one hundred and forty-nine million kilometres away.'

The man started walking again, a little more hurried than before, as if alarmed by the statistic he had heard and the tone of extreme reverence used to speak it.

'Light from one hundred and forty-nine million kilometres away!' Alfredo repeated loudly. He had seen the passer-by in his peripheral vision, correctly guessed the nature of the man's reaction, and been vaguely irritated by it.

'Travelling at an incredible three hundred thousand kilometres a *second*!'

Cente, ask simple questions.

What is light?

Light is a wave of photons that travels at three hundred thousand kilometres a second, until it hits our retina. At that point, light is stopped dead in its tracks and converted into an energy impulse, which is then translated by our brains into an image. This is the one time that light can be seen at rest – when we see it. Although another way of thinking about light would be that it can never be seen at rest. Move as fast as you like, but you'll never catch . . .

This is the problem, Cente. Some questions, even simple questions, have complicated answers. Some things are too complicated to be easily expressed.

Why street kids?

Alfredo asked himself this question as often as his colleagues, friends, family or anybody else. And he didn't really have an answer. Or rather, he had several answers that were neat and well argued, and perfectly rationalized, but were probably not true.

For example. It had been long acknowledged that there was a

difference between Filipino and European psychology, in terms of social structures. Filipino psychology put a greater emphasis on the collective, whereas European psychology put a greater emphasis on the individual. Conveniently highlighting the difference, in the English language 'lonely' and 'unhappy' were two separate words.

So some Filipino psychologists had argued that a direct import of European psychological practices would be problematic, and that a Filipino model would have to emerge from, and take into account, existing traditional practice. However, in the case of street kids, family and community structures could have been non-existent from a very young age, which meant the kids grew up as alienated individuals, outside the group-emphasized collectives.

Here then, surely, was *Why street kids?* There was a gap in the academic studies of street-kid psychology, and Alfredo was filling it. Usually, when asked, this was the reason he would give as the motivation for his research.

Except it wasn't his motivation at all. It was a reason his research might be useful, but it wasn't what motivated him. The gap in research on Filipino street kids might have been comprehensively filled by every working psychologist in the world, but Alfredo doubted it would have interrupted his labours for more than a minute. So, *Why Street kids?* remained.

An alternative explanation: Alfredo had grown up in Ayala Alabang, one of Manila's wealthiest and best-protected sub-divisions. In a city where the void between the rich and the poor was wider than just about anywhere else on the planet, that was saying something. Something, in this instance, about the way opposites attract. About positively charged and negatively charged human particles. About the upper-class fascination with what might have been, but for the hand of.

But no, that wasn't it either. Too obvious, too pat.

Anyway, the real question wasn't *Why street kids?*, it was *Why Cente?* Why was Cente always on his mind?

And the answer, Alfredo knew, was going to be hard to express. If at all, it was going to be found in the statistics of cosmic distances, as bound to complexity as the light from that evening's sunset.

3

Legaspi Towers was a tall building, thirty storeys high, with a glass-fronted foyer, a polite concierge and two express elevators. In the elevators the ride was often shared with late-middle-aged women with painted pink-white faces and gold jewellery. First three floors, shops and boutiques. Fourth floor, admin. Fifth floor, access to an open-air swimming-pool which observed a strict dress code: no shorts or sandals. Sixth floor and above, the apartments, ranging from five-bedroom family flats to one-bedroom bachelor pads. The very top floor was taken over by a single penthouse suite. Alfredo's home.

He walked quickly through the rooms, switching on lights, disturbing the stillness that had greeted him as he came through the front door. Once the whole flat was glowing, he went to the kitchen and poured himself a glass of mineral water. Then he went to the living room, sat heavily on his sofa, and clicked the answer-machine. He had one message.

'Hi, Fredo,' said the machine.

'Hi, Romario,' Alfredo replied blankly.

'Romario here. It's four in the afternoon, so I guess you're still out and about. Doing your stuff. Call when you get back in.'

For the next five minutes, Alfredo didn't move a single muscle, except to blink and breathe.

'So, first I just want to get a few facts about you. A name and an age to begin with.'

'Vincente. I'm thirteen. What about you?'

'Okay, Vincente. Are you sure about that age?'

'Fairly sure.'

'And can you tell me something about how you came to be living on the streets.'

'I came to Manila with my father, from Batangas, and he disappeared. It was about five years ago.'

'Disappeared?'

'I was waiting by some traffic-lights and he never came back.'

'You never saw him again.'

'No.'

'. . . What did you think about that?'

'I wondered where he went.'

'You have no idea about where he might have gone.'

'No.'

'Or what happened to him.'

'No.'

'Okay . . . What about your mother?'

'What about my mother?'

'Uh, well, do you have any contact with her?'

'No. She's somewhere in Batangas. I don't know anything more than that.'

'Other family? Brothers, sisters . . .'

'No brothers when I left. Two sisters . . . I think. I'm not positive. Two or three.'

'Uncles, aunts, grandparents . . .'

'Probably, but it makes no difference. I'm just me.'

'You're just you.'

'Yes.'
'That's an interesting way of putting it.'
'That's the way it is.'

This is the way it is, Cente.

The sunlight travels one hundred and forty-nine million kilometres, at three hundred thousand kilometres a second. As it hits Roxas Boulevard, late in the day, it makes the sky a deep orange. Earlier in the day, scattered differently off the air molecules, it makes the sky blue.

Light can never be seen at rest. Move as fast you like. Start running, and keep accelerating until you're racing across the solar system at two hundred and ninety-nine kilometres a second. Then look at light. Far from having caught up, you'll discover that it is still hurrying away from you at the same frantic speed it was before. Moreover, your brain will have slowed down, and, to an observer not quite able to match your pace, you will appear almost motionless, flattened, and rotated in space.

Return to Earth, and check your watch. It will be set to a different time than those of your friends, family, or anyone you will ever meet.

Or maybe don't return to Earth. Keep going. Nearly four and a half years later, you'll reach Proxima Centauri, our solar system's nearest star.

4

Alfredo found himself in his study. Found himself, because he hadn't intentionally walked in there, sat down, and switched on his computer. As far as he was concerned, he hadn't moved from the sofa and was still staring into middle distance with a bland answer-machine message echoing in his head. The dislocation only became apparent when the computer's screensaver kicked in, and middle distance became a hypnotic swirl of coloured Möbius strips – a vision too extreme to ignore, or pass off as hallucination.

The study was an important area, a place where Alfredo spent a good deal of his time, and had been lit very exactly. A pool of warm light from his desk lamp, bleeding into the corner shadows. An open door, so that the brightness of the living room was close at hand. Open curtains, so that the moon, stars and shining city windows could play a similar role.

The study was also arranged very exactly, though it would have appeared as a stereotype of academic chaos to a stranger. Books and papers on the floor, Post-It notes all over the walls, fat ring-binder folders that haemorrhaged their contents wherever they lay. But naturally, this sprawl of information had a delicate order to Alfredo, in which the slightest interference would have been quickly spotted.

Contrasting with the clutter on the floor and walls, Alfredo's desk was a model of neatness. Apart from the computer and the lamp, only four objects ever found their way on to its surface. The first was a pen, for final editing of print-outs. The second was a tray for unedited print-outs. The third was a tray for edited print-outs. The fourth was a framed photograph of his wife.

It had been taken nearly ten years ago, the day of her nineteenth birthday, six weeks before their marriage. She was wearing a blue T-shirt with the Bench logo emblazoned across her chest. She had a cigarette in her mouth, and was pulling a parodied expression of a sultry American movie-star.

The one other important feature of the study was its hi-fi, and the shelves of diligently labelled, chronologically stacked tapes that sat beside it. The hi-fi was never switched off. All day, all night, the red and green digital displays were in a state of readiness.

Alfredo glanced over at the cassette deck. In the machine was the tape he'd been listening to that morning. One of the earlier recordings.

'I was hiding up a tree, and I had an Armalite rifle. I was waiting for my enemy to walk by, and then I was going to blow him away. A full clip, right in his head. Then I saw him, and he'd captured Josa.'

'Josa . . . The pretty girl who works at the Paradise pool hall.'

'Right.'

'You like Josa.'

'Everybody likes Josa! So, I couldn't shoot my enemy because I'd shoot Josa, so I jumped down, and threw away my gun. He saw me, and tried to attack. We had a fight, but I was too quick, and I managed to escape. But he'd shot me in the fight, and my shoulder was wounded. Luckily I was still able to roll away from the rest of the bullets. This time I attacked him, and I won. I grabbed his gun and shot him, even though I was wounded in the shoulder. Then I rescued Josa.'

' . . . Who was your enemy?'

'Some guy with a moustache.'

'But why was he your enemy?'

'He was dangerous. He was a kidnapper. A professional.'

'And what happened after you rescued Josa? You never really talk about that.'

' . . . Nothing. That was the end.'

'You didn't, say, kiss her, or . . .'

'Kiss her?'

'Kiss her, or whatever. Did she thank you, perhaps? After all, given how often you rescue her from peril, some kind of thanks would be in order.'

'I agree, but there was no kissing. Josa's fairly respectable. Anyway, she dates the Paradise manager, so, what are you going to do? The guy drives a car, for fuck's sake. A Toyota. And he's about twenty years older than me.'

'Okay . . . So . . . was that the only dream you had this week? Or were there any others, more like the ones we talked about last time?'

'Nope. This was the only dream.'

'I see . . . Do you think that next week, maybe you could try to . . .'

'Fredo, why don't you like dreams about rescuing girls?'

' . . . Uh . . . it's not that I don't like them . . . But, we've been talking now for six weeks, and my project is going to last at least a year. I'd just appreciate a little variety.'

'No, that's not it.'

'It isn't?'

'No. Don't you ever dream of rescuing girls?'

'We aren't here to talk about my dreams.'

'We are now. Come on, do you or don't you?'

' . . . I'm not going to answer that question, Totoy.'

'Why not?'

'Well, for my project, it's important that you . . . uh . . . don't know too much about me. In terms of details.'

'How come?'

'Because it might affect our relationship. Even without you realizing it, you might adapt the things you tell me, according to what you believe I want to hear. Or don't want to hear.'

'Hmm. You know, if this is about money, I can give you back one of the pesos you gave me, in return for your details.'

'That's very reasonable of you, Totoy, but I have enough pesos for the moment . . . So, look, I think you ought to try to bring me a different kind of dream next week.'

'And I think you ought to ask yourself why you don't like dreams about rescuing girls.'

'*Do you, now?*'
'*Yes, Fredo. I do.*'

Alfredo tapped the keyboard, clearing the Möbius screensaver, and discovered that not only had he switched on his computer without realizing it, he had opened a file.

C:\docs\PHD\cl.doc

At the top of the page, in underlined bold type, was the Ph.D's title: 'Social Structures in Filipino Urban Juveniles: conscious and unconscious narratives of breakdown and change.'

Beneath the title, italicized, were more personal words: '*Don't just look at me, Fredo! Write me!*'

Alfredo frowned. 'Repetition,' he muttered. A few seconds later he changed the sentence to: '*Stop procrastinating, Fredo! Write me!*'

Rapid Eye Movement

I

'The only way I know to disable the tanks is with this specially constructed grenade.' Vincente looked into Totoy's outstretched palms and saw a collection of nails. Then he looked over at the sluggish stream of cars turning into United Nations Avenue.

'We should choose our target carefully,' Totoy continued. 'There's no point in picking off troop transporters.'

'You don't want to hit a jeepney.'

'Troop transporter.'

'Right.'

'Yes, forget about the troop transporters. We've got to go for one of their latest breed of attack vehicles.'

'An expensive car.'

'Tank.'

'Tank. Okay.' Vincente scanned the traffic jam for a suitable model. 'What about a Toyota make of tank?'

'Mmm . . . No.'

'Daewoo?'

'Uh-uh.'

'BMW?'

'BMW? Jesus, Cente. How often do you see a fucking BMW? We'd be here all night.' Totoy stood on tiptoe, biting his lower lip with stern concentration. Then he jabbed a finger towards a red saloon car. 'No. There's the target. Honda.'

The guy was deep in conversation on a mobile phone. He was in his early thirties. He had a pleasant, healthy, father's face, and was wearing the kind of shirt that suggested he spent most his waking hours in air-con.

And yet he wasn't using the car's air-con now. He had the window rolled down, his shirt-sleeves rolled up, and his forehead was bright with sweat. A cigarette hung from his mouth. Judging by his relaxed posture and his expression of easy affection, he was talking to his wife or one of his children.

'Why him?' said Vincente.

Totoy shrugged. 'Why not?'

' . . . I don't know. Just . . . why him?'

'You need to have a reason for everything?'

'Not everything.'

'So what's your problem?'

'I told you, I don't know. It's like, this guy . . . he's on his way home. He's phoning home now, saying he's stuck in traffic. He's on his way back to his family.'

Totoy studied the Honda and its driver. '*Paré*,' he said. 'The guy is driving a tank, he's radioing for battalions of reinforcements, and if we don't take him out then his army will capture Manila.'

Vincente started laughing.

'You think that's funny?'

'Uh . . .'

'You think Manila being invaded is funny, Cente! Thousands dead? You want that kind of blood on your hands? Because I can tell you right now . . .' Totoy's eyes widened at the prospect of such terrible carnage. 'I don't.'

2

'*You little bastards! Sons of fucking whores! Get back here, you little . . .*'

'Your family ma—' Totoy panted, limbs pumping furiously, fists balled, chin and chest jutting out.

A few moments later he attempted the sentence a second time. 'Your family man has some temper on him.'

'Yep,' Vincente agreed. His longer legs meant that he didn't find the sprint pace such an effort. 'He's pretty angry all right.'

Vincente enjoyed running fast in Manila at night. It felt like the exercise of a skill worth having. Pot-holes, cracked pavements, open sewers, slippery canal-banks, shanty side-streets that shifted and rearranged themselves according to the spread or destruction of slums. Broken glass. Bits of sharp metal with rusted edges. Trip at speed and you could fall anywhere, be cut by anything. You didn't run fast down dark Manila streets unless you were an expert or had no choice.

A couple of years ago, Vincente had been hanging around near Quiapo bridge, not doing much, when a man ran past. The type with a job and a briefcase, not unlike the driver of the Honda they had just nailed. For reasons that were not apparent, he was being chased down by a seven-strong gang. There was a gap of about thirty feet between the pursuers and their quarry.

Vincente hadn't needed to witness the end of the chase to be sure that the guy hadn't escaped. The uncertainty was whether he'd been killed or not. You had to feel bad for him.

But at the same time, you had to feel good for yourself. Vincente knew that if he had been in the man's shoes, the thirty-foot gap would have given him a fighting chance of avoiding capture, and probably allowed him to get clean away.

*

'Getting tired?' asked Vincente.

Totoy shook his head, because he was too short of breath to speak.

'You mind if we keep jogging a little while?'

Totoy's head shook again, so they kept going.

They fell into a compromise rhythm that took into account the differences in their sizes and length of stride. While they were running, a roughly equal distance was maintained between their shoulders – or, for that matter, any chosen point on their bodies. Every time one of them looked to the side, he saw his friend in the same space he had been occupying before. In fact, relative to each other's position, the two boys barely moved at all.

But around them, the neighbourhood changed.

3

Who'd shoot a cat?

A wealthy college boy, using the pocket-sized automatic his old man had given him on his eighteenth birthday. He occasionally told a story about once having fired it in anger, but when questioned he fudged the details and pretended it was a subject he didn't like to talk about. In truth, he had never fired his gun in anger, which, for reasons he genuinely didn't like to talk about, was something that bothered him.

One night he was riding his motorbike, hurrying across town to meet a girl in a Makati bar. His route took him through the barren streets around the ruined Hotel Patay. As he turned on to Sugat Drive, off Sayang Avenue, a cat suddenly appeared in his headlights. The shock made him brake hard, and the bike slid from under him, skidding across the road in a shower of sparks. Picking himself up, shaken and furious, he saw the cat that could have cost him his life, and had certainly fucked up his motorbike.

Half a minute later, his story about having fired his gun in anger acquired a ring of authenticity. The details would always remain fudged, but at least his cheeks wouldn't burn while he fudged them.

A drunk cop in a black pit of depression, driving his squad car down what once had been a red-light area, a gold-mine of drop-dead teenage whores and backhanders in his younger days. Pulling the car over to the side of the road, he gazed at the deserted buildings, stared down alleys that should have been neon-lit. Overwhelmed by nostalgia and beer, his eyes filled with tears. 'I'm a dying breed,' he whispered hoarsely. 'I'm yesterday's man.'

At that moment, a cat strolled into view. On impulse, the cop drew his revolver and shot it. After watching the cat bleed to death, he dried his eyes with his forearm and bit the cap off another bottle of San Miguel. Then he put the car in gear, eased away from the kerb, and continued his slow journey down memory lane. Before the next hour was up he had shot himself.

A woman whose kid died of septicaemia, the result of a scratch from an ill-tempered stray. Driven insane by the loss, she walked the streets seeking revenge, marking the cleansing kills with notches on her pistol's wooden grip.

A wired shabu-smoker, feeling invulnerable and punchy at the world, ready to prove it to anything that moved.

A cat hater. A mouse lover. A rat protector. A gangster's chauffeur.

4

'I don't care who shot it,' said Totoy. He was lying spread-eagled on the pavement, and when he sat up, the perspiration from his shorts and T-shirt left a neat imprint on the kerbstones. 'I'm too tired to care. I never ran so far in my life.'

Vincente squatted by the bundle of blood and fur, twirling his fingers in the curls of hair that had survived the Barangay Tanod. 'I care,' he said. 'I think it's strange. It's hard to think why anyone would want to do something like that.'

'I could stay here the whole night, and not move again.'

'I mean . . . it's a cat. How could you get so angry with a cat that you'd want to shoot it?'

'I'm serious. I could go to sleep on this very spot. I'm that tired.'

'If there were houses around, you'd think it might be because the cat was wailing, and some guy wanted to get to sleep. But nobody lives around here.'

'I'm thirsty too. I need something to drink.'

'If you touch it, it's still pretty warm.'

'You want to find a Seven Eleven? See if we can sneak past the guard and nick a Coke?'

'Poor cat . . .'

'Mmm, a Coke . . . Refreshing and delicious!'

'Just one of those things, I guess.'

'*Coke,*' said Totoy impatiently. Vincente cupped one of the cat's paws in his left hand, ran his thumb over the retracted claws, and shook his head.

Conversations with Vincente were not always easy. He was liable to talk about weird stuff, and he also had a habit of getting stuck on a subject, so that for a fortnight or more he could hardly talk about anything else. A few months ago, the subject had been hell.

It wasn't official, not a rule, but the deal was that if you took the food from the soup kitchen, you got a sermon. The Irish priest would limp over to where you sat in the canvas-tent canteen, dragging behind him the leg that had been damaged in his Mindanao missionary days. For a short while he'd watch you chew your rice, and if you glanced up, he'd give you a wink and a small smile. Then, about three or four mouthfuls from the bottom of the bowl, he'd clear his throat and – in his accented but extremely fluent Tagalog – begin.

A typical opening line would be: 'I'll tell you a thing, boys. Sit tight and listen to this thing. I was lying awake in bed the other night, as I sometimes do, when a peculiar idea struck me. Only God knows where paradise is. To us, to you and I, the location of paradise is an eternal mystery. And yet, with equal mystery, we know exactly how to find paradise. We don't know where it is . . . and yet we can find it. It's an interesting thought, is it not? Perhaps we could dwell on that a short while.'

But this evening, the chain of events took a different turn. Just as the priest was about to hit the throat-clearing stage, Vincente cleared his.

He said: 'I'm in trouble. I'm going to go to hell, padre.'

'Oh,' the priest replied, apparently more surprised by Vincente's readiness to chat than by the words themselves. Silence was usually the reception he got from his soup beneficiaries. '. . . Well, I'd say you are altogether too young to have come to such a conclusion. Perhaps you could tell me how you reached it.'

'It's an idea I have.'

'A foolish idea. I've known you long enough, and you're a good boy. Much too good for the devil.'

'I still think I'm going to hell.'

'I see.' The padre knotted his fingers together, presenting an archway of chewed nails. 'Vincente . . . is there something you've done? Perhaps it would be something you'd rather talk about in private, just the two of us. We could go for a walk, or . . .'

'It's something I'm *going* to do. Not something I've done.'

'You plan to sin?'

' . . . I don't see how I'll avoid it.'

'But son, this is why the Church is here for you. To provide the means and guidance by which . . .'

'Hell,' Vincente said, 'goes on for ever. It never stops. And once you're in, you can't get out.'

Judging by his expression, the priest didn't appreciate the interruption, but he took it in his stride. 'That is correct, Vincente. The torments of hell are never-ending.'

'If my dad is dead, do you think he's in hell?'

' . . . Your dad?'

'Is it a possibility?'

'I . . .'

'Does anyone go to hell?'

' . . . Yes.'

'So it's a possibility.'

'If he's no longer with us, you could say it's a possibility. But . . .'

'I think he might be there because he abandoned me. I think he might be being tortured by devils.'

'If I go to hell, I'm going to become a devil,' Totoy cut in abruptly. He'd noticed something in Vincente's voice, a sudden cold flatness, and knew it was a precursor to trouble. Potentially a precursor to being banned from the soup kitchen. 'I'm applying for the job as soon as I arrive.'

'Now, Totoy,' the priest chided. 'You wouldn't want to be a devil for a minute. Devils are barred from the gates of heaven, and therefore suffer the same torment as damned souls.'

'I think he might be being tortured by devils, padre,' Vincente repeated, completely undeterred by Totoy's attempt to move the discussion to less volatile ground. He put his bowl down, even though his soup wasn't finished yet. 'He's in hell, and he can't get out. I don't think it's fair.'

'There must be quite a lot of devils,' said Totoy, his anxiousness increasing. 'Hell must be huge.'

But now the padre was as undeterrable as Vincente. 'Fair is not something you worry yourself about,' he said with the authority of personal experience. 'To find fairness in life, you would have to know the mind of God.' Then, in illustration, he tapped his knuckles on his bad leg.

'I'm not trying to find fairness in life. Hell is after life. And I don't think it's fair that God decided to put my dad there.'

'Vincente, if your dad is in hell, which is something neither one of us could know, it wouldn't be because God put him there. Quite the opposite. By deciding on our actions in life, we decide the nature of our afterlife.'

'Nobody would *decide* to go to hell.'

'You might say that nobody would *want* to go to hell, but . . .'

Vincente interrupted the priest again. 'If God has put my dad in hell, the only way I'd ever get to see him again is if I go to hell too.'

'Ah,' said the padre. 'It seems I'm being slow on the uptake. Now I see where this is going.'

'You think hell has visiting days?'

'Son, a moment . . .'

'I doubt it does.'

'Son . . .'

'So if I do nothing wrong in life, I don't get to see him again. And if I do something bad, I get to see him, but I also go to hell for ever.'

'Son! Would you listen a moment!'

'Does that sound fair to you?'

'As I have already said, to find fairness in life you would need to know the . . .'

'Jesus *Christ*!' Vincente exploded. 'I'm not asking about the mind of God or your fucking leg! I'm asking *you* if it sounds fair!'

The priest looked stunned. 'I . . .' he said.

'Don't ban us from the soup kitchen!' said Totoy.

'Yes or no would do it, padre!' Vincente shouted furiously, getting to his feet. 'How fucking hard can that be?'

The priest was an understanding and merciful man, so neither boy was banned from the soup kitchen, despite the swearing and the food fight Vincente's hurled bowl precipitated.

'Don't worry, son,' the padre said, when Totoy went to see him the next day, full of profuse apologies on his friend's behalf. 'Of course you can both come back. You can come back any time, and you'll be made welcome. In the grand scheme of things, a food fight isn't too bad . . . though I'd be very grateful if it didn't happen again.'

He then added, 'And, just so as you know, I had a word with the Lord late last night. You aren't going to hell, Vincente isn't going to hell, and his dad isn't either. You tell Vincente that. I don't want you boys fretting about devils and the like, you hear?'

Totoy assured him that he wouldn't fret about devils. And he didn't.

Vincente, however, did. Every night for two weeks. What could you do? That was his nature.

Totoy sprang up off the pavement.

'I'm telling you right now, Cente, I'm not going to spend the next month talking about how that cat got plugged. Okay?'

Vincente paused. 'Let's find a Seven Eleven,' he eventually said. 'I could use a Coke after all that running.'

5

There were no Seven Elevens. There was nothing. And walking seemed to lead nowhere, though there was no sense of retracing footsteps. Each boy privately wondered how they'd found their way to these streets in the first place. Particularly Totoy, who hadn't been lost in the city for as long as he could remember. Getting lost was as unexpected as forgetting how to swim, mid-dive into the Pasig.

Vincente, for his part, was more bothered by the area itself. It was confusing to have stumbled across such uninhabited desolation in Manila. Not that desolation was a rarity, but you would find people living in it.

Equally confusing, it was clear that the area had once – perhaps even recently – been full of life. The evidence was everywhere, in filth-blackened shop-fronts, peeling fly-posters and busted neon signs. Moreover, peering inside the buildings, bizarre details appeared. Through broken windows, restaurant tables with place-mats and beer bottles could be dimly made out. One derelict bar even had a juke-box. It lay on its side, dusty but apparently intact, surrounded by crumpled drink-cans and torn newspaper, like a Japanese treasure chest in a sea of cursed banknotes. It was hard to imagine why such reusable and recyclable assets had been abandoned, rather than expertly stripped. It seemed as if, in the space of one bad hour, the night-life had been chased away.

A similar thought had obviously occurred to Totoy, embellished with a characteristic spin.

'I'm keeping an eye out,' he said quietly, after they had gone the entire length of a street without conversation.

Vincente raised his eyebrows. 'For?'

'The clown.'

' . . . What clown?'

'The burger clown. I'm thinking he might be the reason this district is so deserted. Could be his hunting-ground.'

Vincente was content to let the oblique reference pass unexplained. He was feeling uneasy enough, and didn't need a grim Totoy fantasy to help him on his way.

The stretch of wasteland came as a relief. It was illuminated by a few scattered refuse fires and the moon, and beyond it an outline of low shanty buildings was visible. Some had lights burning, electric and oil.

'Looks promising,' said Totoy. 'The squatter camp . . .'

'Uh-huh.'

'We could ask someone the way back to Ermita.'

'Nothing to lose.'

'So . . .'

' . . . We might as well try it out.'

6

Half-way across, Totoy said, 'It's pistols.'

Vincente nodded.

'Loud.'

'Near.'

'Coming from inside a building.'

'One of those ones behind us.'

'Yep.'

The boys stood still and listened. The shooting came in rich volleys, and its echoes bounced off the buildings around the wasteland, snapping through their chests.

'That shot was louder.'

' . . . Somebody's screaming.'

Rescuing Girls

I

Like walking from the living room to the study, and switching on the computer. Like walking from the desk to the window, and frowning at pinpricks of old light. Underneath '*Stop procrastinating*' he had typed: '*Imagine an atom of hydrogen.*'

Imagine an atom of hydrogen, Cente. The most basic atom: a nucleus with a single electron revolving around it. Then imagine that you have enlarged the nucleus by five million million, bringing it up to about the size of a one-peso coin. To scale, the electron would now be nearly one kilometre away.

A kilometre between nucleus and electron, if the nucleus was the size of a one-peso coin. In an atom, almost nothing to see, even if you could see it. Mainly a void. So much room to move around.

So much room that if you fired a neutrino into a light-year-thick block of lead, there'd be even odds that the neutrino would collide with nothing and pop out the other side.

Good odds of survival, if you are a light-year-thick block of lead, trying to blow your brains out with a neutrino gun.

Good odds of survival too, if you are a suicidal neutrino, jumping off the thirtieth floor of Legaspi Towers. You'd hit the pavement and pass straight through it. Pass through the pavement, earth, rock layers, the whole planet, and keep right on going.

Good odds of suicide survival for the unthinkably big and the unthinkably small.

You might hope that the same would be true for a girl jumping off the thirtieth floor of Legaspi Towers. With all that space, with all that void and room to move around, you might hope the girl's atoms and the atoms of the pavement might conspire to let her safely through.

It seems reasonable enough. But it turns out that, for the thinkable, the odds are bad.

Alfredo wiped sweat off his top lip. 'Stop,' he said, and hit delete.

2

Alfredo decided to ignore today's Totoy tape. At some point, he would have to go through it more carefully, when he was dealing with the conscious narratives of breakdown and change, rather than the unconscious ones. But for the moment, he couldn't be bothered. Instead, as usual, he chose to concentrate on his star pupil – to the extent that Vincente was the pupil, at any rate. In neat capitals, he labelled Vincente's tape, '#43, Dying/dead baby, careless father'.

The conversation was still quite fresh in his mind, so rather than listen to it immediately, he thought it might be better to go over some previous father-related material.

'Father, father,' he muttered, squatting by the shelves, running his finger down the Vincente recordings. Out of forty-three taped conversations, there was a lot of father-related material to choose from. At #4, his finger dithered, and at numbers 5, 6, 9, 11, 16,

17, 18, 23, 24, 28, 30, 31, 36 and 37 it dithered again. Finally it backtracked, and settled on '#29, Running man (version 2)/ father-hell'.

'. . . It's not the first time you've brought me this dream.'

'No. But it's the only dream I could remember this week.'

'I see . . .'

'Do you not want to buy it?'

'. . . Why would I not want to buy it?'

'You complain about Totoy's dreams always being the same.'

'That's a little different. Actually, I'm interested that you've had this dream more than once.'

'Oh, well, I've dreamed it a lot more than once.'

'Regularly? Every week, month . . .'

'Sometimes I have it every week. Sometimes I might not have it for a while.'

'And for how long has this been going on?'

'I'm not sure. About a year.'

'About a year . . . Really . . .'

'Why?'

'Well, we've been seeing each other for about a year. And while you were talking about the dream, you mentioned that it was based on a real incident. But you also said that the incident happened two years ago . . . so I'm wondering why the incident has suddenly become important to you.'

'Hmm . . .'

'Tell me why you think it might be important.'

'You tell me.'

'I'd like you to try first.'

'Fredo, we've been talking for ages today. I'm tired. And I want to find Totoy before it . . .'

'. . . Gets dark. Okay. So . . . it struck me that the man lacks a kind of street knowledge, and for that reason you are sure he will be *caught by the street gang. And in a way, you feel good that if you were in his shoes, you would be able to escape.'*

'Uh-huh.'

'You also emphasize that this man is quite well dressed, and he's carrying a bag with him.'

'Yes.'

'So . . . doesn't that make you think of something? Or someone?'

'No.'

'Come on, Cente! It must make you think of someone.'

'It makes me think about the guy I saw being chased.'

'Fine. But someone else too. Look, we've been seeing each other about a year. Then, in the last year, you start having this dream about a guy who lacks street knowledge, is well dressed, carries a bag . . . Why are you laughing?'

'You. You think the guy is you.'

' . . . Is that such a funny idea?'

'Well dressed?'

' . . . I'm expensively dressed.'

'You are?'

'I . . . What about the bag?'

'It was a briefcase. Not a sack.'

'This isn't a sack!'

'It certainly isn't a briefca—'

'Shit,' said Alfredo, hitting the pause button on the tape deck. He counted the rings on the phone, feeling irritated with himself that he'd turned the answer-machine off. After twenty rings, it became clear that Romario wasn't going to give up.

3

In general terms, they shared nothing but a school, and that had been long ago. They liked wildly different music, films and books. Romario talked in clipped, blunt sentences, while Alfredo tended to discover what he was saying while he was saying it. Alfredo had been born into money, and Romario had made it. When Romario had been sowing his wild oats, Alfredo had been married. When Romario had found the love of his life, Alfredo had stumbled out to his apartment balcony to find himself loveless.

For these reasons and more besides, the friendship, whenever it was analysed, left both men in a state of mild surprise. This was reflected in the amount of time, over the years, they'd spent discussing how they had met, and why – after having met – they hadn't immediately turned around and walked off in opposite directions.

For a few seconds, Romario seemed too disgusted to speak. Then he said, '*Paré*, what's the point of pretending you're out, when you know I can see your apartment lights from my office.'

Alfredo stalled with a cough. ' . . . I forget that, *paré*.'

'*Bullshit,*' Romario barked. 'You don't forget at all. You want to know whether I'll keep ringing or not.'

'Sorry.'

'It's like the way you never phone. You *never* phone! Who phones who? Always it's me who phones you.'

'I'm sorry.'

'You want my opinion? You're testing me. If I didn't phone, I'd fail the test, and you'd probably leave it six months before you got in contact.'

'No, paré,' said Alfredo firmly, settling himself down on the sofa and tucking the receiver under his chin. 'I wouldn't leave it six months. But that's good about the test. You're probably right.'

'Of course I'm right.'

'Maybe you should've been the shrink and not me.'

'Maybe.'

' . . . You pass the test. I'm glad you keep calling.'

'You should be.'

Alfredo smiled. 'I am.'

'Good. Now wait while I put you on hold.'

' . . . *We're going to be right back with a track from two guys who are currently rewriting the Pinoy techno rule-book, taking on the Makati venues with style. You know who I'm talking about, straight out of Cardona Rizal, turn it up and flip to this . . . right after a short message from Burger Machine, that's the twenty-four-hour burger, the burger that never sleeps . . .*'

Other people's offices played Casio-keyboard Bach & Dr Hook covers, but in Romario's office, callers on hold were tuned into Flip FM, Manila's only round-the-clock non-stop-dance-music station. That was because Romario owned and ran Flip FM.

'Did you know,' Alfredo had once asked Romario, 'that the radio waves from Flip FM will travel deep into outer space? A few million centuries from now, you could be reaching a whole new target audience of alien life-forms.'

Romario had been nonplussed. 'That's great, Fredo,' he had replied. 'I like long-term strategies. But at the moment I'm more worried about reaching life-forms in Ilocos Norte. When I can transmit a half-decent signal to Northern Luzon, I'll get back to you.'

'Right,' said Romario's voice, breaking into the rewritten Pinoy techno rule-book, whatever on earth it was. 'I'm considering

Japanese. I got drunk last night. I'm feeling ill. I'd like to eat some Japanese.'

'Food?'

'Yes, you are a funny guy. So what about it? We could all get some Japanese.'

Alfredo paused. 'All?'

'All. Me, you, all.'

'All is more than two people. All implies others.'

'Mmm . . .' Alfredo heard Romario rearranging some papers. 'So, *paré*, how about it? Japanese!'

'Just me and you?'

The papers were rearranged again. 'Mmm . . .'

'Romario?'

'What?'

'Me, you, and who else?'

'Uh . . . Well, it'll be me and Sylvie.'

Alfredo closed his eyes. 'And Sylvie is bringing . . .'

'I don't know. Why does it matter?'

'A girl.'

'No, a box of fucking Dunkin Donuts. Yes, a girl! I think she works for the *Inquirer*. So pretty you can't believe she hasn't been snapped up. Face like an angel, and bright too. Reads books.'

'Romario,' Alfredo said.

'Oops,' said Romario. 'I've got to go. Last meeting of the day just turned up. Now, Fredo, here's what you have to remember. I'm going to be in the office for the next forty minutes, and then I'm going to leave for the restaurant. If you're going to come, call me and I'll pick you up in the car. If not, you're a prick, and I'm going to be failing your stupid test pretty soon.'

Alfredo said 'okay' to the dead line.

4

'*This isn't a sack!*'

'*It certainly isn't a briefcase.*'

'* . . . Fine.*'

'*Not that it's a bad bag.*'

'*But it's not a briefcase.*'

'*Sorry.*'

'*Nothing to apologize about.*'

'*You look a little offended.*'

'*Offended? No, not at all.*'

'*And the running man . . . he wasn't you. I mean, I understand what you're saying, about how he could have been you. Like a few weeks ago when I had the dream about a cat, and you said the cat might be Totoy. I could see that. There was something about the cat that did kind of remind me of Totoy.*'

'*But the running man didn't remind you of me.*'

'*Right.*'

'* . . . So perhaps he reminded you of somebody else.*'

'*Well, that's what I was just about to say. It seems to me that, if anyone, the guy was like my father.*'

'*Uh-huh. Can you tell me why?*'

'*They both died the same way.*'

'*If your father died, Cente.*'

'*He died, and he died like that. I think he must have been in a stick-up. He got chased, and same as the running man, he didn't know what to do. So he got caught. That's how I see him dying.*'

'*Hmm.*'

'*Do you think he died that way too?*'

'* . . . That's a tough question. I think that, from what I know about your life, it is possible that your father is dead. And I suppose that if he did die, it's possible he died like that.*'

'Good. I thought you were going to try to talk me out of it.'

'. . . I wouldn't do that. I do want to say that it's impossible to know what happened to your father . . . but being realistic, it might have happened the way you describe.'

'Yes.'

'It's extremely sad.'

'Sad.'

'Don't you think?'

'Depends who for. It's sad for him, because he must have been scared before he died. But . . .'

'. . .'

'. . .'

'. . . But?'

'I don't know. Totoy gets to see his mother once or twice a week, and she's a mess. Have you ever seen Totoy's mother?'

'No.'

'She's never clean. She's thin, there's about ten white scars on her face, and people tell her she's got AIDS. And when she dies, she's probably going to go to hell because when she was begging, she drugged Totoy's little sister to make her look sick. But she over-drugged her, and she died. So with me and Totoy, who has it better? When I look at his mother, I think at least I don't have to see my father like that. He isn't in a gutter, covered in shit. And in my memory of him, he was a good father, so he isn't in hell. He's in paradise, which means I guess I'll be seeing him again some day, as long as I don't . . .'

'. . .'

'What?'

'. . . Sorry?'

'That look you just gave me. What was it?'

'Did I give you a look?'

'You looked at me in a strange way.'

'I did?'

'Yes. When I said about paradise, and seeing my father again.'

'. . . Can you tell me what was strange about the look?'

'It was like you thought I was wrong.'

'What about?'

'About seeing him again.'

'. . . Oh.'

'You do think I'm wrong. I can see it in your face right now.'

'. . . No.'

'No? So look me in the eye, and tell me I'm going to be seeing my father again in paradise.'

'Uh . . .'

'Why can't you do it?'

'It isn't my place to say such things.'

'You agreed with me about how he might have died.'

'. . . This is a little different.'

'You don't have to say a word now! It's obvious what you're thinking. I don't get it, Fredo. Do you know something I don't?'

'. . . What do you think I might know?'

'Cut it out. I don't want to play these question games at the moment.'

'I'm not playing a game, Cente. I want you to try to answer the question yourself. What do you think I might know?'

'I'm not sure.'

'Take your time.'

'You . . . You think I'm not going to see my father in paradise, which either means I'm not going to be there, or it means that . . .'

'. . .'

'. . .'

'Cente?'

'It's got dark. I said I wanted to stop talking before it got dark. Now it's got dark.'

'. . . You have to find Totoy.'

'I have to find Totoy. We're going to the soup kitchen tonight. I've got to go right now.'

'Okay . . .'

'Can you give me the money, please.'

5

Alfredo took the tape out of the deck, put it back in its case, and lay down on the floor. The carpet felt soft under his head, a plastic ring-binder felt hard under his left leg, scattered papers rustled and slid when he stretched out his arms.

He thought: sorry, Cente.

Sorry. Your talk of hell threw me. I could have given you better answers.

This is the way it is. Galaxies drift away from each other like painted dots on an expanding balloon, and hydrogen atoms have a single proton. There are hundreds of millions of hydrogen atoms in a single drop of water. Galaxies contain hundreds of millions of stars.

Nine planets orbit our star. We are not at the centre of our solar system, and our solar system is not at the centre of our galaxy, and our galaxy is not at the centre of the expanding balloon.

Totoy's mother isn't going to hell, she's in it. Your father isn't in hell, because nobody is. And he isn't in paradise, because nobody's there either. When a street gang chases you down unfamiliar streets, when you hit the pavement outside Legaspi Towers at two hundred miles an hour, nothing happens.

QED

I

The slum on the far side of the wasteground was a haphazardly constructed maze of reclaimed wood, plastic sheeting and corrugated iron. Once they had run inside, orientation was impossible. The only constant was the sky, wheeling above as they swung lefts and rights down walkways that were sometimes barely wide enough for even their narrow shoulders.

They tried various directions and strategies, taking turns to lead the way. If Totoy's route was taking them closer to the action, a tapped arm gave immediate and unargued deferral. If Vincente was so confused that they had circled the same few alleys three times in four minutes, a tugged sleeve passed control.

But no matter what they tried, the hunt was all around. It panted behind them, growled ahead, and to their sides they heard it smashing its heavy flanks against the walls of the squatter shacks. All around, and always near. Just as escape seemed possible, a short burst of shooting would crackle from within a twenty- or thirty-metre radius. So they would double back, aiming away from where they thought the shooting must have been, and find themselves breathing gunsmoke.

Vincente grabbed Totoy's T-shirt sleeve, and held it fast. Totoy slowed.

'I don't want to keep doing this,' Vincente hissed. 'If we keep doing this, we're going to run into them. If we're running, they might shoot us.'

Totoy's head flicked around the compass points. 'Okay,' he whispered.

'I think they'll shoot anything that moves.'

'I'd like to climb a wall. We'd be safe up a wall.'

'There isn't a wall to climb. We should just stand still. We aren't the ones they want. We should stand still, let them by.'

'You want us to stand still . . .'

Vincente nodded.

'So . . .' North, South, East, West. 'We'll do that. Stand still, let them by . . .'

It didn't take long. A man arrived like a three a.m. timber-truck, crashing out of the dark, filling the world. And he disappeared as quickly as he had appeared. But not forwards, speeding past in a rush of violence and fear – he disappeared in a clattering and splintering of gangplanks, downwards.

There were quiet seconds following his fall into the open sewer trench, before he erupted back up again in a spray of thick liquid, his howl inaudible to the boys through the pounding bloodstream in their ears. Then he was out of the sewer, and gone.

The two men in suits tore past a few moments later.

2

The 'cano who had fallen into the sewer was finished. His size and his automatic pistol weren't going to do him any good. He was going to be caught by the two men in suits and they were going to shoot him dead – this was his destiny, however you cut it. There was only one other thing worth bearing in mind. Anybody in the path of his destiny could wind up dead too.

And Cente knew that. After all, it had been Cente who suggested that they stop, stand still, and let the chase go by. So Totoy didn't understand what was going on. When the two suits had run past, he hadn't even had time to say 'Phew' before Cente lit up like a Chinese firework and set off in pursuit.

Totoy wanted to wrestle him to the ground and ask him what his fucking game was, *joining* the chase just as they'd been given the opportunity to get *away* from it. But it was hard enough to keep Cente in sight, let alone leap on his back. In fact, Cente was moving so fast it seemed that rather than trying to follow the suits, he was trying to overtake them.

Plenty of questions, but no time to give them consideration. Between keeping Cente's T-shirt in view, straining his eyes in the darkness, and concentrating on where his feet were landing, Totoy's attention was fully occupied.

Or – almost fully occupied. There was one small part of his head that had decided to go on a wander. It was surprising and a little irritating, but he didn't feel there was much he could do about it. In a strange way, he felt as if his head was too occupied to bring itself to heel.

The wander had begun with the rhythm kept by his feet, to the extent that his feet were keeping a rhythm. One-two, one-two-three, one-two-three-four . . . Then the numbers had become words, and the words had become a chant, and the chant had progressed to a memory.

'You can't keep the fucking rhythm! What the fuck is the matter with you?'

'Well, I'm not a girl, am I?' Totoy shouted, picking himself up and pulling the tangled length of rope from around his legs. 'Do I look like a girl? Am I wearing a skirt?'

'You think only *girls* skip?'

'You ever seen any boys skip?'

'Boxers skip! Prize-winning boxers in the Olympic fucking games!'

'Boxers don't *skip*!'

'Yes they do! You think you're better than boxers? Too tough to skip!'

'That's right!'

'Ha! A teeny prawn like you, and you're tougher than Olympic boxers with prizes!'

'Yes!'

'Ah, fuck you!'

'Fu–' Totoy picked up the rope and threw it in his mother's face. 'There!' he yelled, and began marching away.

She let him take about ten paces before she called him. 'Hey, Tots,' she said. 'Don't sulk. Skipping is difficult at first, but you'll get used to it.'

'I'm not *going* to get used to it,' he replied over his shoulder.

'I just thought it would be fun, but we don't have to skip if you don't want to.'

'Fun,' said Totoy, with the kind of distaste he usually reserved for invoking the names of notoriously dangerous policemen.

'Come on, Tots. I never see you, and it's nice when we do stuff together. Like a proper family.'

'Proper family!' Totoy let out a great hoot of derision. 'You remember what the last thing you suggested we do together was?'

'Don't bring that up again!' his mother wailed. 'You weren't going to actually get screwed by the guy! We'd have slit his throat long before it got to that stage!'

'So if you *had* pimped me to the fat Australian, then we *wouldn't* be like a real family. But you were going to *kill* him before he got his dick out, *so it's okay*!'

His mother wrung her hands. 'Tots, Lord knows how many times I've said I was sorry for that *terrible* idea. Can't you forgive me?' She watched Totoy as he half-turned towards her. 'I was drunk for fuck's sake!' she added plaintively, and smiled when he started walking back.

They sat in the shade of one of the bus terminal's shelters and shared a cigarette. Usually, Totoy didn't smoke – he had dabbled with butts until he was eleven, and never acquired the taste – but on this occasion he smoked with his mother because she'd offered him a rare Champion blue-seal from a pack, and he knew how much that must have meant to her.

'Ah,' she said, drawing deep on the menthol. 'It's like a cool sea-breeze. One day, Tots, I'll take you to the village where I grew up. Then you'll know what a real sea-breeze is like.'

'That will be good,' said Totoy agreeably, thinking that the day his mother took him to the provinces would be the day hundred-peso bills rained from the sky.

'You'll meet your grandparents, if they're still alive, and your uncles and aunts. You'd like your aunts and uncles. And I'm sure there would be plenty of cousins for you to play with . . .' She sighed and tapped ash. 'That's all I ever did when I was your age. Play.'

'Skipping, I suppose.'

'You wouldn't know it to look at me now, but I was always the best at skipping. I could do it the fastest and I could twirl around so my skirt lifted up. The other girls would get tired and barely be able to say the chant, but not me! I could sing the chant as loudly as I liked, twirl around, and still spy on the boys playing basketball.'

'So,' Totoy said drily. 'The boys were playing basketball.'

'The boys didn't skip because they were too scared! The chant frightened them all to bits.' His mother laughed and pinched his cheeks with her bony fingers, bringing the tip of her cigarette worryingly close to his eye. 'That's probably why you flew into such a rage. The chant scared you!'

He shrugged. 'It was a pretty weird chant. All those people being eaten.'

'Oh, but it had to be scary, Tots . . .' From the last drag before the filter, his mother paused to blow a neat smoke-ring. 'If it hadn't been scary, there'd have been nothing to stop us tripping.'

3

Totoy was wrong. If Vincente had wanted to overtake the two suits, it would have been no problem at all – he'd gained on them quickly, and increasingly broad alleyways had presented him with the option to pass several times. But Vincente didn't want to overtake them. He didn't want anything. He had an impulse to tail the chase, and beyond that, he had no plan.

No plan, and only one worry.

'Don't follow,' Vincente panted, though Totoy was much too far behind to hear. Every time Vincente glanced back, the small shadow would be struggling along, just able to stay in sight.

'Stop following. I'll meet you later by the Ermita McDonald's. We'll work customers on their way out . . .'

For their part, the two suits seemed less concerned by their own shadow. Neither gave any impression of knowing it was there.

The shit-covered white man led his pursuers out of the slum and into a wealthier area. Once in it, although the terrain made for easier running, their sprint speed dropped to a jog, as if they were taking time to appreciate the pretty scenery rather than battling with leaden calves and short breath.

To Vincente, the blossom that lined each side of these streets looked like the Mount Pinatubo ash-fall.

Which was appropriate, he immediately commented to himself. Pinatubo had erupted seven months into his year of silence, the midway point between his father's disappearance and Totoy's leap from the Intramuros tree. He had heard the news in a traffic jam, walking past cars in which every radio was tuned to the same bulletin. Days later, ash from the explosion was still drifting down over Manila. The grey flakes had filled the air, coating the branches of trees, collecting in drifts by the roadsides.

Vincente almost smiled to think how much the observation would have pleased Alfredo, if this had been a dream. He would have asked, 'Did the dream feel like a nightmare?'

'Sure.'

'You woke up feeling . . .?'

'Bad.'

'And what do you think the dream might mean?'

'I know what you think it might mean!'

'Go on.'

'You think the blossom is ash, and the running man is my father, and Totoy is following because he's going to save me, jumping down from the Intramuros tree.'

'. . . Yes. You are absolutely correct. And as usual, your perceptiveness has confounded all my expectations, no matter how often I revise them. I should be used to it by now, Cente, but I'm not. I can never predict what's going to come out of your mouth. You're an endless surprise.'

'You always say that.'

'Well, what do you want me to say? You always surprise me.'

'Give me my money, please.'

'Exactly. QED.'

*

Vincente nearly jogged into the two suits' backs. Looking beyond them, down thirty or forty metres of sodium-lamp light-pools, the running man had stopped running.

4

Vincente expected the suits to continue towards the man without breaking stride, then kill him quickly. But instead they immediately split apart, crossing to opposite sides of the road, and were now inching forwards along the grass verge at a half-crouch. They were offering the man the same respect you'd offer a cornered animal. Vincente matched the new careful pace, but stayed in the middle of the road.

Vincente had taken ten short steps. He tried to imagine what the man was thinking, on his hands and knees, staring at tarmac.

The man answered by suddenly rolling over to lie flat. His gun veered in the rough direction of the suit on the left, then to the suit on the right. On the next sweep, it hesitated on the small central target.

Vincente wondered why the man hadn't started firing. Perhaps hitting people in darkness at such distances was more difficult than it seemed. Perhaps his magazine was empty, or had only a couple of bullets left.

The gun veered away again.

A soft patter of footfalls indicated that Totoy was closing.

Vincente felt a strange pressure swell in his chest, a hand that had reached inside him to grip his heart. He turned to the suit on the right. The suit was wearing a torn and black-stained shirt. 'Why don't you shoot him?' Vincente asked, pointing towards the man. 'Are you out of bullets too? You should shoot him now.'

For the first time, the suit acknowledged the boy's presence. He replied, 'Kid, who *are* you?' Then he looked angry, and said, 'This isn't a game! Get the fuck out of here!'

Vincente turned to the suit on the left. The suit on the left returned the gaze without any expression in his eyes or face. 'Stick around, kid,' he said, 'and you'll get killed.'

Vincente didn't know if the suit was asking him to stick around or if he was delivering a threat. 'I'm not playing a game,' he said, and the pressure subsided.

The man had more fight left in him than his broken posture on the road had suggested. He scrambled up and started stumbling across the front yard of a house.

Now, finally, the two suits opened fire.

The man screamed, or cried out, and jumped head first through what turned out to be a kitchen window.

Supersymmetries

I

Alfredo slid open the French windows of his living room and went to stand on his balcony. The fingers of one hand were curled around the guard-rail. In the other hand, he held the framed photograph from his desk. The lights of the city clustered and moved, cars and bedrooms, curtains drawing, blinds lifting, buildings etched in pinprick vectors. These lights lit the night cloud layer, and the city was darker than the sky above it.

From the thirty-storey perspective, in the cubes and rectangles, in the pinprick vectors, in the isometric conjunction of a shopping-centre complex and a low office block, Alfredo searched for and found a particular shape.

Cente.

Take six cubes and arrange them into the shape of a crucifix. Take two more cubes and stick them either side of the crucifix, at the point where the cross is made. Now you have a tesseract. A tesseract is a three-dimensional object. A tesseract is also a four-dimensional object – a hypercube – unravelled.

A square unravels to a line. Two dimensions unravel to one.

A cube unravels to a cross. Three dimensions unravel to two.

A hypercube unravels to a tesseract. Four dimensions unravel to three.

You exist in three spatial dimensions. In the same way that a one-dimensional boy could not visualize a two-dimensional square, or a two-dimensional boy could not visualize a three-dimensional cube, you cannot visualize a hypercube.

A hypercube is a thing you are not equipped to understand.

You can only understand the tesseract.

This means something.

For you and for me, Cente, this is the way it is. We can see the thing unravelled, but not the thing itself.

2

It's early evening. A pot of chicken stew is ready to be warmed up on the cooker, and a pot of rice sits beside it. You're standing on the balcony of our apartment, leaning against the guard-rail, taking in the view. Cente is in the living room, reading a book on the sofa.

Every so often he looks up to check on you. Sometimes you see him looking, and you give him a little nod. He nods back or gives you a smile, and goes back to reading.

Then he sees something in the book that he thinks you'll find interesting. It's a popular-science fact of the kind you like so much. A semiprecious science jewel, a useful side-piece of the jigsaw, a big thought for a short pause.

Cente says your name to get your attention, and reads the paragraph out loud so you can hear. He makes an effort to speak clearly, and tries to convey the enthusiasm he feels for the idea behind the words.

When he finishes, he remains staring at the page. He knows that if he looks up from the book again, you're not going to be there. At some point over the minute it has taken him to read the paragraph, you will have jumped, slipped, fainted or fallen.

It's a dream.

Cente stares at the page for as long as I'll sleep that night.

3

Alfredo imagined letting the framed photograph drop from his hand. As he pictured it, he could have followed the path of its descent for six or seven storeys. The last he'd have seen would be a bright flash as the protective glass cover caught the light of a passing window. Past that, the distance between the top of Legaspi Towers and the pavement would be far too great to discern whether the photograph hit the ground or passed right through.

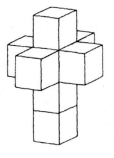

The Tesseract

'Okay,' Sean said.

He was shot in the chest twice. The force of the bullets did not throw him backwards; his legs simply folded and he collapsed on to the kitchen floor. On the floor, a third bullet hit him in the thigh.

For several seconds, Sean didn't think of anything. He was aware only of turbulence. As far as he knew, he had fallen out of a plane, been struck by a car, been swept overboard by a wave, or tripped down a flight of stairs. The turbulence had no history and no future. It was a pocket of violent surprise. If somebody could have spoken calmly to Sean during these few seconds, he would have accepted any suggestion as a plausible cause for his confusion.

When his mind began to clear, Sean was left with an overwhelming sensation of limited time. Time for his mind to have and complete a single, final, thought.

Through the strobe of images that followed this sensation, a girl's face resolved itself. She didn't have a face that would have launched a thousand ships, and she had no enigmatic smile. But she was honest, solemn, and Sean knew she was there to protect him from whatever she could.

Lito

In the light of the oil lamp, with the sheen of sweat, her solemn face looked like polished bronze. Lito pressed four fingers of rice into a ball and popped it into his daughter's mouth. She screwed up her eyes and spat it out. 'Not nice?' he said, and she shook her head.

Lito sighed contentedly. Every night of Isabella's pregnancy he had lain awake worrying about what form their baby's abnormality would take. And when the baby had been born, and a careful inspection of her body had revealed perfection, his alarm had increased. He could only imagine that the abnormality lay on the inside: a missing lung or damaged heart, a crucial defect in some other vital organ.

So when, after the milk stage, her abnormality turned out to be that she refused to eat rice, he had nearly died of relief. Yes, it was endlessly problematic, given that rice was on her parents' menu three times a day, and the volume of fried potatoes she consumed made Lito feel ill if he stopped to think about it. But her freakish diet didn't seem to have stopped her growing into a healthy and beautiful three-year-old girl.

'Spat it out again?' said his wife's voice behind him.

Lito brushed a mosquito off his daughter's leg. 'Yep,' he said.

'Lito, if you want her to eat rice, you should stop trying to force it on her. If you stop trying to force it on her, she'll come round. Take it from me.'

'No, Isabella,' said Lito tersely. 'Take it from me. She won't.'

'If you tried . . .'

'Isabella,' Lito interrupted. 'That's enough.'

Isabella let the matter drop. Her husband was a sweet-natured man, but he could get oddly fierce when it came to discussing their daughter's eating habits. A blessing in some ways, that

Lito's one area of short temper concerned something as inconsequential as rice.

'It's hot,' said Isabella, to change the subject. 'Nights like this never seem to end. So hard to sleep.'

'True,' Lito agreed, after a short pause. 'Maybe we should sleep outside tonight.'

Isabella nodded, pleased to hear her husband's voice returning to a less abrasive tone. Then she walked over to the doorway of their nipa hut.

Through it she could see the silhouette of Lito's boat, pulled up on the beach beyond the high-tide mark. Beyond the boat, moonlight caught the swell on the sea. Beyond the sea, a strip of electric lights glowed on the mainland like a broken necklace.

The lights of barrio Sarap, one mile distant from their small island.

Raphael

Through the kitchen doorway, Raphael saw his grandmother on the floor of the kitchen, bleeding like the victim of a jeepney accident. Beyond her, framed by the broken glass of the window over the sink, he saw the head and shoulders of a boy.

The boy had a ragged shaved haircut and a filthy face. Raphael wondered who this boy was, where he had come from, and why the glass had been broken in the first place. He felt sick and cold with fright. He clenched his hands to his bare chest. Under his fingers, he felt the hard delineation of his scars, and hoped that he wasn't about to be burned again.

A man appeared over the head of the boy. At once, there was an explosion of shouting. Amid the voices, he heard his mother. Her voice was lower and quieter than the others, but more urgent.

The shouting continued, strange barking words that he didn't understand.

The shouting stopped. He heard a man talking with his mother.

Then there were three loud bangs. Raphael felt a clawing blow on his head, tugging him backwards, and everything went black.

Sonny

'Gotcha,' said Sonny, and stood up to admire his handiwork. Somehow, the newly replaced tyre made his car look more complete than it had before the puncture. More complete, and more his own.

Similarly, the grease and dirt on his shirt and hands pleased him. It had been too long, he decided, since he had got himself scuffed up in such a way. Another decision quickly followed: the coming Saturday, he would take Raphael to the Megamall. They'd eat a pizza or some kind of American fast-food, maybe see a film, do a little window-shopping, and then – springing the kind of surprise that earns permanent credit in the good-dad bank – they'd buy a bike.

A bike. Stabilizer wheels that would eventually have to be removed, jogging down Baluti Avenue with his palm in the small of Raffy's back, the application of sticking-plasters to small brown knees, the changing and mending of flat tyres.

Sonny felt like telephoning Rosa at once to tell her the plan. She could take Lita out on the same day, and buy her an appropriate girl's treat. Could be a dress, he speculated, or some jewellery.

'Lita's first necklace,' he said. 'Gold.'

For another minute, he remained gazing at the Honda – which

now looked to him as if he had built it bolt by bolt, from scratch. Then he took his mobile from his trouser pocket and began dialling his home number.

But just as he was about to key in the last digit, Sonny changed his mind. This was the sort of plan that was best not explained over the phone, particularly if Corazon was hanging around in the background – which she certainly would be. Better to tell Rosa later, when they were lying together in bed, her head nestled against his left arm. That would be the best time.

Sonny climbed back into his car, started it up, and waited for the chance to pull into the stream of traffic.

Teroy

Teroy stood against the wall on one side of the broken window. Jojo was next to him. Between him and Jojo was the street kid.

This weird kid, chasing them around.

'You want a gun?' Teroy said.

It was a sort of joke. He wasn't going to give a gun to the weird kid. Who knew what was going on in his head. He was probably crazy.

'You want to see stuff?'

Teroy grabbed the kid with his free hand and hauled him around so that he stood directly in front of the broken window.

'There. Now you see everything. What do you see?'

No reply.

'I know you can talk. What do you see in there?'

No reply still, but the kid wasn't getting shot or shot at.

Teroy spun around, raising his gun over the kid's head, pushing forwards to sandwich him hard. He didn't want the kid moving or being a distraction.

Through the window was a kitchen. The English man was in the kitchen. He was holding a woman against him like a shield. There was an older woman bleeding on the floor.

Teroy didn't shoot because he didn't want to kill the young woman. And the English man didn't shoot, maybe because he didn't want to shoot the kid, but more likely because he didn't have any bullets.

'Drop your gun,' Teroy shouted to the English man.

The English man shouted back in English.

'Move your fucking head,' Teroy shouted to the woman. 'Move your head and I'll kill him.'

Corazon

Corazon's body worked to keep itself alive. Making decisions that were beyond any decision-making process, congealants tried to stop the flow of blood from the entry and exit bullet-holes in her side, muscles stiffened around the wounds.

Meanwhile, Corazon slipped in and out of consciousness. When conscious, she would notice that she was sprawled on the kitchen floor. This disconcerted her, but no more so than if she had woken to discover she had slept in a twisted position, meaning a day ahead of grumbling complaint from a stiff neck.

While unconscious, however, her mind was more troubled. She dreamed that a black dog had leapt into her daughter's house and was preparing to eat the family. Worse yet, if anything could be worse, she had a strong feeling that she had brought the dog to them herself, either by having failed to prevent its coming, or more likely by a past word or action. A misjudgement, a mistake, that had chased her for years and come to this.

'*Perro negro, perro mío, Dios mío,*' she prayed ardently. '*Por favor, dé su protección a esta casita y esta familia.*'

But the prayer was confused and as misdirected as her guilt, and it went unheard.

Mercifully, the dream was fractured. It never quite ran through to its terrible ending. If not interrupted by a few seconds of consciousness, it looped back on itself, returning Corazon to the moment she first glimpsed the dog, sitting on the road outside, about to turn its gun-barrel gaze to meet her. So she was spared all bloody conclusions, except, eventually, her own.

Don Pepe

Don Pepe's mouth was red and dry where a bubble of blood had popped over his lips, his eyes were rolled up in their sockets, and his fingers were curled into claws.

In the Spanish town of San Sebastián, a restaurant owner recalled a memory of the rudest customer he had ever served, an old man with an unplaceable accent and a linen suit that looked as out of its time as his silver matchstick-dispenser. In Quezon province, the young nephew of a Manila dockworker shuddered at a story about red mists and machetes. In Negros, a cemetery caretaker shone his flashlight on the graffiti-covered walls of an old Kastila mausoleum. In an Ayala Alabang mansion, six Dobermanns licked their paws and listened for the sound of a Mercedes engine.

These fragments, and others like them, were the form in which the *mestizo* continued to exist. Together, they represented his life as inadequately as a shoal of milkfish represents the South China Sea. In this respect, death had reduced him in precisely the way he had feared it would.

Lita

Lita knew exactly what to do. She reached around Raphael's head, clamped her hands over his eyes, and yanked him backwards. She was much bigger and stronger than Raphael, so he couldn't resist.

She pulled Raphael so forcefully that his weight crashing into hers sent them tumbling to the hallway floor. Even as they fell, Lita kept her hands over Raphael's eyes. When they were both on the floor, she rolled him on to his front, trapping him beneath her. Her knees held his legs and her elbows held his arms.

It was a grip that ensured Raphael was blinded, contained and protected. Lita felt as if she had known these actions under these circumstances, this drill, for as long as she could remember. She had learned it from her parents, coded into her through years of witnessing the way they watched him, the way they spoke to him, even the way they put him to bed.

Lita kept Raphael held tight until the shooting had stopped and she heard her mother calling their names, at which point she felt that the danger had passed, and it was safe to let him go.

Jojo

Jojo heard Sean say 'Okay.' Immediately, Teroy began shooting over the street kid's head. Teroy fired three times, then he shoved the boy out of the way, and began climbing through the window.

Jojo dropped his pistol.

The boy stumbled to the side, then took a few uncertain steps away from the house. He was holding his ears – Teroy's gun had gone off only a few inches from his head – and he looked as if he was having difficulty keeping his balance.

Jojo walked over to the boy, who was now turning slow circles on a single spot on the driveway, and took one of his wrists. Jojo's fingers closed so completely around the thin forearm that it felt as if he were making a fist.

'Sit down,' he said. The words were hard to say. His tongue felt thick in his mouth and his head felt as if it were full of smoke. When the boy gave no response, Jojo pulled the wrist downwards. 'Kid, sit down here. You'll feel better soon.'

The boy sat, then laid himself out flat. From inside the kitchen, Teroy's gun fired three or four times more. With each gunshot, the boy twitched. To Jojo, it looked as if the boy were being shot himself.

'Hey, hey,' Jojo said. 'Relax. You're not hurt.'

A lady in the house cried out.

'You aren't hurt,' Jojo repeated, and he knelt down. ' . . . I still don't know what you're doing here. I can't imagine why you chased us, but I hope you had a better reason than me.'

This comment produced a response of a kind, though it was ambiguous what the response might mean. The boy's eyes flicked towards Jojo's, then at the sky.

'I don't think I had any reason to be here at all,' Jojo continued. 'If you were to ask me why I came here, I'd say I came here because I did. I'd say, that's just the way . . .'

Jojo frowned.

In his smoke-filled head and out of his thick-tongued mouth, Jojo heard his father's voice.

'That was the way it was.'

His father, speaking like a priest. A red mist, rising like steam off cane cutters' backs in the early morning. A stooped figure in a doorway, smelling like the split husks beneath coconut trees.

Reflexively, his thumb turned the wedding band on his left hand.

'This is over,' Jojo said, standing abruptly. 'I'm alive. I'm going home.'

Then he went to help Teroy, who was clambering awkwardly out of the kitchen window.

Totoy

Three more gunshots from inside the house, followed by the sound of screaming and crying. Most of the screaming and crying was a kid, Totoy noted blankly.

A few moments later, a man – one of the two suits – climbed out of the front window. As he climbed out, a part of his clothing seemed to catch on the broken glass in the frame. Maybe it cut through the clothing to his skin, because he suddenly jerked sideways, which made him slip, and he fell to the ground.

The second of the two suits helped him stand. Then both men walked down the driveway, passing Totoy without a second glance, and began jogging down the road, back in the direction of the slum.

Totoy walked up to where Cente lay in the driveway of the house.

'I tried to keep up,' he said, squatting beside his friend. 'You were so fast, you left me behind. My legs are too short to keep up with you when you run so fast.'

Cente didn't look as if he were listening. He was staring at the sky, tight-lipped and unblinking, as he had done earlier when Totoy had jumped him from the scaffold.

'Are you winded?' Totoy asked. 'Or angry?'

Cente remained impassive.

'Why are you lying down?'

The noises from inside the house distracted Totoy for a couple of moments. The crying had intensified, for no clear reason. When he returned his attention to Cente again, his friend had closed his eyes.

An idea crossed Totoy's mind. A little tentatively, he lifted Cente's T-shirt and put a hand on his chest. Cente's chest was warm and wet only with sweat, and under the ribcage was a heartbeat.

'Phew,' said Totoy, removing his hand. 'For a moment, I was afraid you might be dead.'

He hesitated, then added, 'The shooting,' by way of explanation. 'With all that shooting, I was afraid you'd been killed.'

Inside the house, the crying abruptly stopped. Now the street and the night seemed very quiet.

'But you aren't dead,' said Totoy. He lay beside Cente and folded his arms behind his head to act as a pillow. 'You're just thinking.'

Alfredo

Alfredo had stopped thinking. He closed the French windows to the balcony, sat down on his sofa, and picked up the phone. Then he dialled, agreed to hold, and listened patiently to Manila's only twenty-four-hour dance-music station.

Romario didn't leave him holding for long. 'So?' he said.

'So,' Alfredo replied, 'the larger the searchlight, the larger the circumference of the unknown.'

'What?'

'The last words I spoke to my wife. Or at least, it was the last line of the paragraph I was reading. I couldn't say for certain whether she heard it or not.'

Romario cleared his throat. 'Oh,' he said.

'Did I never tell you that before?'

' . . . No.'

'Well, there it is . . . Anyway, pick me up.'

' . . . You're coming to dinner?'

'Yes.'

'You are?'

'Yes.'

'Jeez,' said Romario. Then, down the phone line, Alfredo heard the sound of a briefcase clicking shut. 'Fredo, stay right where you are. I'll leave now. I'll get over to you in about fifteen minutes.'

'Fine.'

'This is great! Sylvie will be really pleased, and you're going to like her friend a lot. She's just the sort of girl you need to . . .' Romario paused. 'Fredo, you'd better not change your mind on me.'

'I won't,' said Alfredo. 'Call on the car phone when you pull up outside. I'll come down.'

'Fifteen minutes.'

'Sure,' said Alfredo, and began to put the phone down.

'No, wait!' said a small voice, just as the receiver was about to hit its cradle.

Alfredo lifted the receiver back up again.

'Do something,' said Romario.

'Do something?'

'Uh . . . you've got to make yourself look nice. Have a shower and put on some fresh clothes. Some good clothes. Have you got time to have a shower in fifteen minutes?'

'I'd have thought so.'

'Then have a shower.'

'All right.'

'Good clothes! A clean shirt!'

'Yes.'

'Fifteen minutes!'

'Yes,' said Alfredo. This time he disconnected the line with a push of his finger.

Rosa

The armed Filipino outside the kitchen window shouted that Rosa should move her fucking head so he could kill the man behind her.

The Englishman shouted, '*I'm going to die. I'm covered in shit. I fell in a fucking sewer.*'

The Filipino gunman repeated that she had to move her head.

'*I'm going to die in this fucking kitchen, covered in shit.*'

'Move your head!' the gunman shouted a third time.

'I can't move my head!' Rosa shouted back at him. 'Please don't shoot! You've already shot my mother! There are two young children in this house! Please don't kill them!'

Something indefinable seemed to change in the gunman's expression. He said, 'Your children are not going to be killed.' Then his mouth closed and he didn't shout at her again.

Rosa blinked. Her mind was working slowly, but her thoughts were clear enough. '*Is it possible for you to shoot over the head of the boy?*' she asked the Englishman quietly.

'*How can I?*' he answered in half-sob. '*I don't have any fucking bullets left.*'

'*Then,*' Rosa said, '*in a few moments, unless you let me go, he will kill us both.*'

The man sucked in a sharp lungful of air before replying. During this time, Corazon expelled a loud sigh.

'*Okay,*' he said.

*

He let Rosa go. Rosa threw herself to the side. The man stood alone for half a second, arms bunched to his side, pointlessly tensed in defence. Then he was shot.

Rosa slid to the floor and covered her eyes.

She could hear the Filipino gunman climbing through the window.

'You said my children wouldn't be killed,' she whispered.

A crunch of glass told her that he had jumped down from the kitchen sink, and was in the room.

'Please,' Rosa said.

She uncovered her eyes and saw the gunman standing over the dying Englishman, firing into his head. The gunman fired until his pistol was empty. Each explosion caught her breath like a hiccup. The final shot made her scream.

While Rosa screamed, the gunman reloaded and the Englishman's blood spread quickly across the floor. She continued to scream until she dimly realized that the gunman was waiting for her to stop.

The scream tapered away.

'That's your mother,' the gunman said, gesturing with his free hand at Corazon's body.

Rosa didn't know how to respond.

'I'm sorry she's dead,' the man said flatly.

She nodded.

The man nodded back. 'Sorry,' he said again, in the same oddly polite, emotionless voice. Then he walked to the sink, hauled himself up, and was gone.

'Lita,' Rosa called. 'Raffy.'

At once, two reassuring wails burst out from the hallway.

'Kids, don't come into the kitchen. Everything is . . . stay in the . . .'

Stay? The word sounded ridiculous. What for? Stay until she

had a chance to clear up the mess, slide Corazon and the shit-covered foreigner out of the way somewhere, mop the floor? What difference would it make?

Rosa sat in the blood and glass, alternating her gaze between the two corpses.

She told herself: take a minute to think. I should recognize this territory by now. This is the aftermath of dynamite, and it is familiar to me. I know what to do from here.

She tried again.

'Lita, Raphael, stay where you are.'

Vincente

Vincente lay beside Totoy on the tarmac. He wasn't dead, he was thinking.

He had chased a running man, and seen what happens when a running man is caught. In the house, he had seen a young boy, about the same age he had been when his father disappeared. He had seen a sink; plumbed in, a good sink, the kind of sink you get in a good house.

He thought: there should be something here that I am meant to understand.

Vincente thought harder.

Some time ago, Fredo had talked about thinking.

'When you say, "I just thought of something," what you mean is, "I just stopped thinking of something." You've been having the thought for a while, turning it over in your mind, developing it, without realizing you were doing so. Maybe for days or weeks. Maybe even years.'

Vincente thought: the running man wasn't my father, the boy wasn't me, I can't be sure if I ever had a sink like that or not.

Maybe there is nothing here I am meant to understand.
Maybe there is no meant to understand.
This means something.
Vincente stopped thinking.

A car pulled into the driveway. Vincente and Totoy sat up, squinting into the bright headlights until the driver switched them off. Both boys recognized him, but he didn't seem to recognize them. He stared over their heads with a puzzled expression.

Up and down the blossom-lined road, figures stood in lit windows. In one front garden, a man in shorts and a vest held a shotgun, watched from the doorway by his wife. No further than five blocks away, a police siren rose and fell.

'We'd better go,' said Totoy quietly as the Honda driver ran past.

'Rosa?' yelled the driver. 'What the hell is going on?'

'We'd better,' Vincente agreed.

As they hit the street, they heard a woman's voice behind them and the driver's sudden gasp of alarm.

'God!' he exclaimed, as if his faith had been punched out of his body.

Totoy looked back over his shoulder and Vincente didn't.

Author's Note

Some definitions of a tesseract describe it as a hypercube unravelled, and others define it as the hypercube itself. I chose the version used here only because I happened to prefer it. Similar liberties have been taken with everything presented as fact in this novel.